Someday

Someday

 Jackie French Koller

SCHOLASTIC INC.

New York Toronto London Auckland Sydney
Mexico City New Delhi Hong Kong Buenos Aires

ACKNOWLEDGMENTS

The author wishes to thank the employees of the Quabbin Visitors
Center and the members of the Tuesday Tea group for their help in
researching this book. Deepest appreciation goes to the former
residents of the Swift River Valley who shared their memories with
her—in particular, Lois Barnes, who shared not only her memories
but also her time and knowledge as expert reader for the manuscript.

ISBN 0-439-44087-4

12 11 10 9 8 7 6 5 4 3 2 1   3 4 5 6 7 8/0

Printed in the U.S.A.   40

First Scholastic paperback printing, January 2003

The text of this book is set in 11.5 Goudy.

Book design by Helene Berinsky

*For all those
who loved, and lost,
the Swift River Valley*

Someday

1

February, 1938

I had always known, of course, that the reservoir was coming. Folks in Enfield had been talkin' about it long as I could remember—after church on Sundays, at the grange hall pot-luck suppers, at husking bees, barn dances, community sings. . . . Whether you were standing in line at the post office or waiting your turn down at Haskell's General Store . . . just about anytime, any place you got two or more Enfielders together, you could be sure there'd be tongues wagging and fingers jabbing over the coming of the Quabbin.

To me, though, it was always one of those *someday* things that you don't tend to worry about too much when you're a kid. Like *someday* you'll grow up. *Someday* you'll leave home. *Someday* your parents will get old and die. And *someday* the Metropolitan District Water Supply Commission will flood the Swift River Valley, and the towns of Enfield, Greenwich, Prescott, and Dana will be no more.

Little did I know on that sunny February afternoon, as I sat staring out of the schoolroom window, that *someday* was waiting for me down at the post office, like a silent tiger, ready to pounce.

It had been snowing most of the day, and the schoolhouse was stifling, as usual—the big, wood coal stove in the back corner cranked up as if we were a class full of eggs that someone was determined to hatch. I was sweating and itchy in my woolen dress and kneesocks, longing to be outside catching icy cool snowflakes on my tongue. I glanced up at the clock. Forty-five minutes until dismissal. Why, I wondered, was the last hour always the longest?

To pass the time, I stared out the window and started making up similes about the snow. I'm going to be a famous writer someday, you see, like Lucy Maud Montgomery or Louisa May Alcott, and of course, writers can *never* have enough similes and metaphors, so I've been collecting them for some time now.

"Like grains of rice spilling from a hopper," I wrote in the margin of my open geography book. Not bad. I stared out the window again. "Like dandruff shook loose from God's head," I scribbled. Oh, I *liked* that one.

Suddenly I heard an engine start and noticed a truck pulling out of the alley next to Hesse's Meat Market. As it rumbled by, I saw that it was a moving truck and my heart sank. So now the meat market was gone too.

"Cecelia?"

I snapped to attention. Miss Rourke was standing with her rubber-tipped pointer in one hand. At her back was a map of the world.

"Yes, Miss Rourke?"

"Would you please come up and show the class where Madagascar is?" Miss Rourke asked.

My face started to burn.

"Madagascar?" I repeated.

"Yes. Madagascar. You *have* been paying attention, haven't you?"

"I . . . yes, ma'am."

I saw Chubby Miller trying to hide a grin as I stood and made my way to the front of the room. Chubby is my best friend, and he knows what I'm thinking even before I do half the time. He knew I was up the creek without a paddle.

I took the pointer from Miss Rourke's hand and stood, darting my eyes around the map, scanning for countries starting with *m*. As an eighth grader, and one of the best students in the class, you can imagine how important it was for me not to look like a dumbbell in front of the younger children.

"It certainly is a big world, isn't it Miss Rourke?" I said, stalling for time.

Miss Rourke nodded patiently but didn't reply.

"One can hardly fail to be impressed," I went on, "with the very vastness—"

Miss Rourke rolled her eyes. "Cecelia," she interrupted, "you've been spending too much time with your friend Anne Shirley. Kindly spare us any further discourse on the magnitude of the world and show us where we might find Madagascar."

Some of the students started to chuckle, and I could feel my ears burning. I must admit that *Anne of Green Gables* is my favorite book and that I do tend to identify with Anne a bit, especially since we both have the curse of red hair and freckles. I could see that Anne's gift for gab wasn't going to help me out of this one though. I glanced over my shoulder at Chubby, who gave a quick nod toward the upper left-hand corner of the map.

My eyes honed in on the area he had indicated. "There," I said, pointing to a likely looking *m* word.

The class burst out laughing, and Miss Rourke folded her arms and gave me a look that made me feel like a puppy who'd just relieved himself on her foot. I glanced back at the class and saw Chubby laughing loudest of all. My eyes narrowed. He'd set me up, the bum.

Miss Rourke took the pointer from my hand. "This," she said, pointing to my *m* word, "is Magadan, Cecelia. It's part of the country of Russia." She turned to the class. "Would anyone care to show Cecelia where *Madagascar* can be found?"

A dozen arms shot into the air, and just to further humiliate me, I'm sure, Miss Rourke chose Maggie Blake—a *fifth* grader!

Maggie ran up, grabbed the pointer, and smugly indicated an island off the southern coast of Africa—about as far from Magadan as you could get and still be in the world. My face was undoubtedly the color of my hair.

"Thank you, Maggie," said Miss Rourke. "That will be all."

Maggie flounced triumphantly back to her seat, her ruffled petticoat swaying like a duck's downy behind. Snooty Belinda Wilder gave me a smug grin. Since the Kramer twins had moved away, Belinda was the only other girl in the eighth grade, and we were about as opposite as two people could be. I made a lemon-sucking-priss face at her behind Miss Rourke's back.

Miss Rourke turned around and caught me. I wiggled my face around, pretending I had an itchy nose.

"I suppose, Cecelia," said Miss Rourke, "that you have a good explanation for your lack of attention to your geography lesson."

"Um . . . well . . ." I stalled a moment longer, then sighed. "I'm sorry, Miss Rourke," I said. "I just couldn't resist the temptation to stare out the window. All that lovely snow is such a distraction." I glanced longingly at the window, then turned beseeching eyes upon Miss Rourke. "It looks rather like dandruff shook loose from God's head, don't you think?"

The corners of Miss Rourke's mouth began to twitch, and I knew there was a smile in there trying to get out. Miss Rourke always *did* have a very hard time trying to be stern with me. She'd lived just up the street from me most of my life, and she used to baby-sit for me when I was small. I was allowed to call her Kathy then, and she treated me like a little sister. *Then* she went off to teachers college and came back all grown up and serious. I was sure Kathy was still inside Miss Rourke, though, just beneath that stiff, schoolmarm exterior. It wasn't so long ago, after all, that she'd been a kid in that very same schoolroom, and you couldn't tell me her eyes hadn't wandered to the window a time or two. . . . In fact, they wandered there as I watched, and then they seemed to go all faraway and melancholy.

"Are you all right, Miss Rourke?" I asked.

She blinked and looked away. "Yes," she said quickly. "I'm fine."

But she didn't seem fine. Come to think of it, she'd been sort of quiet all day. How could I have known . . . how could any of us have known, that she had picked up *her* letter before school.

2

"You may return to your seat, Cecelia," Miss Rourke said at last. "Next time, I trust you will try harder to stay focused on your work."

"Yes, ma'am," I assured her. "I most truly will."

Miss Rourke waited until I was seated, then she took up her pointer again. She cleared her throat, glanced out the window once more, and then a mischievous smile stole across her face.

"Now, class," she said, pointing to the United States, to a spot smack-dab in the middle of New England, "this is the Swift River Valley, where it is snowing today. And if you look closely, you can see a tiny one-room schoolhouse filled with hot, tired students, longing for a breath of fresh air. And if you listen closely, you will shortly hear a joyful shout ring out, for their teacher is about to turn to them and say . . . Class dismissed!"

For a second or two we all stared at the map in puzzled silence, then it dawned on us what she meant.

"Leapin' lizards!" I shouted. "She's lettin' us out early!"

"Yahooo! Yippee! Hooray!" others shouted out.

We exploded from our seats, smacking into one another like carnival bumper cars in our rush for the coatrack. And who was right smack in the middle of the pack but Miss Rourke!

"Last one out is a rotten egg!" she shouted, giggling like the old Kathy I used to know.

Like a herd of stampeding buffalo, the lot of us thundered out into the alley between the school and the town hall. In a flash, dozens of little noses were pressed to the classroom windows on the first floor of the town hall. The students in the first through fourth grades had heard our racket.

"Let 'em out! Let 'em out!" We motioned to their teachers, and sure enough, just a few moments later, a torrent of small-fry gushed out through the big double doors of the town hall.

I scooped up a handful of snow and squeezed it in my fist.

"Perfect for packing," I announced.

"Snowman!" someone shouted.

"Yeah!" I yelled. "Let's make the biggest snowman Enfield has ever seen!"

Soon there were kids rolling balls of snow in all directions. Chubby and I got a big one started, and the other four eighth-grade boys—Frank Hopkins, Tom O'Leary, Orville Tate, and Stu Maroney—all pitched in to help. Belinda Wilder stood on the sidelines posing, as usual, in her fur-trimmed hat and muff. I've always hated her because she's beautiful. That's uncharitable, I know, but it's the truth. It's very hard not to hate someone who has creamy white skin and golden Greta Garbo hair when you yourself have a freckled nose and red frizz that can only be tamed by twisting it into braids.

"I'd help," Belinda twittered as we all grunted and shoved, "but Mother says I must always be mindful of my delicate constitution. I might faint if I tried to push that heavy thing."

The boys grinned at her goo-goo eyed. I gave her the raspberry.

"C'mon," I said. "Let's get this thing into the center of the green." The snowball had grown to at least five feet across and weighed a ton, but the boys and I put our backs to it and wrestled it into place.

Not to be outdone, the seventh graders rolled up another ball, almost as big as ours. It took the lot of us to heave the one up on top of the other, but when it was in place, our snowman body stood a good eight feet tall!

"Leapin' lizards!" I cried, huffing and puffing. "I bet no one's ever made a snowman this big! It won't melt till July!"

A pack of little kids rolled up a smaller ball. "Look! We made the head," they clamored.

"Swell!" said Chubby.

"I'll run over to Haskell's and get a carrot for a nose," said Miss Rourke. "Who wants to come? I might have enough change left over for some lemon drops."

"Me! Me!" cried a number of the little kids. Miss Rourke led them off across the green.

Chubby picked up the head and stretched up on his toes, but his reach fell short of the top of the snow body. That posed a dilemma, because Chubby was the tallest boy in the class.

"So, how do we get it up there?" he asked.

"Let's get a fire truck!" Tom O'Leary's little brother shouted.

I laughed. "That'd be keen, Billy," I said, "but I don't think the volunteers'd appreciate us calling them out to help us build a snowman."

"How about a ladder?" someone else suggested.

"Good idea," said Chubby. "We can borrow one from the Feed and Grain."

"The Feed and Grain closed up just after Christmas," I reminded him.

"Oh, yeah." Chubby nodded, then shook his head. "This place is starting to feel like a ghost town."

A number of us paused and looked sadly at all the boarded-up storefronts along Main Street. For a moment our high spirits flagged, but then Chubby gave a shout.

"Hey," he said, "forget the ladder. We'll find another way."

"Hey, Chubby," said Frank Hopkins. "How's about you kneel down and I climb on your back?"

Chubby eyed Frank's considerable girth. "How's about *you* kneel down and I climb on *your* back?" he countered.

"No way, Miller," said Frank. "You'll break my spine."

"I'll give it a try," said Stu Maroney. "I don't weigh much."

Chubby eyed Stu, then nodded. He handed over the snowball and dropped to his knees. Stu climbed up on Chubby's back and heaved the snowball upward, but his reach was still a bit short.

Obviously there was only one person for the job—the second tallest person in the class—me.

"Give it here," I told Stu. "I'm taller than you."

"You?" said Stu. "You're too scrawny to hoist this thing."

"Try me," I said.

Stu handed the head over, and the weight of it nearly pitched me forward onto the ground, but there was no way I was going to back down. Not in front of the whole school, and especially not in front of namby-pamby Belinda.

I climbed up on Chubby's back and took a moment to get my footing.

"Oof," he said. "Puttin' on a little weight lately, Wheeler?"

"Go cook a radish, Miller," I said.

I sucked in a deep breath and shoved upward with every ounce of strength in my body. The ball reached the snowman's shoulders, then I gave it a shove. It rolled over and fell off the other side.

PHLUMP! It smashed to the ground.

"Nice play, Shakespeare," Chubby muttered.

"Jeepers creepers!" Belinda twittered. "You ruined it!"

I turned to her. "Close your yap, Wilder," I said, "or I'll ruin *you*."

"Cecelia!"

Miss Rourke had returned with the carrot. "That was not very ladylike," she chided me. "Now, apologize to Belinda this minute."

I looked at Belinda and grimaced. "Sorry," I grumbled, turning slightly so she could see that I was crossing my fingers behind my back. She stuck out her tongue.

"Belinda!" said Miss Rourke.

Belinda turned red. "She had her fingers crossed," she tattled.

Miss Rouke rolled her eyes. "Honestly," she said, "sometimes I think you girls are worse than the boys. You're going to miss each other now that . . ."

She stopped short and we both looked at her.

". . . one of these days," she added quickly. "Then you'll be sorry for all this nonsense."

Belinda and I eyed each other doubtfully.

Frank and Tom had patched up the head. They handed it back to me, and I stepped up onto Chubby's back again. I sucked in a big breath and heaved it up until it was carefully balanced on the shoulders, then I gave it just the tiniest push. It rolled neatly into place. A cheer went up as my breath whooshed out of me.

I jumped down and stood, grinning proudly at the snow giant.

"We need some arms," I said.

"I'll go find some branches," cried Maggie Blake.

"I'll help you," said Miss Rourke.

"We'll need eyes too," said Chubby.

"Coal!" said Belinda. "The town hall has a coal furnace. I'll go ask Mr. Janes for a couple of pieces."

"Won't you get your muff dirty?" I asked sarcastically.

"I'll help her," said Frank.

"Me too," chimed in Tom. Orville and Stu tagged along as well.

I frowned as Belinda sashayed off, followed by her admiring throng.

"Don't *you* want to go too?" I asked Chubby. "She just might need all five of you to help carry those *heavy* lumps of coal."

Chubby chuckled. "I think she can manage," he said, but

it was clear that his eyes were following Belinda's wiggling hips.

I snorted. "Go ahead," I told him. "I don't care if you're lovesick over her like every other boy in school."

"I am not lovesick over her," said Chubby.

"Why not? She's beautiful. Anyone can see that."

"And you're jealous," said Chubby. "Anyone can see that."

I huffed. "Well, why shouldn't I be? Look at her."

"You're beautiful too," said Chubby, "in a . . . wholesome kind of way."

I smirked. "Oh thanks," I said, "you mean like Bran Buds."

Chubby laughed. "Come to think of it," he said, "you do remind me of Bran Buds at times."

"Oh yeah? Like when?" I asked.

"Like when you give me a pain in the arse," he said. "Like now."

"Talking about a pain in the arse," I said. "I owe you one for that Madagascar business."

Chubby laughed. "I knew Miss Rourke couldn't get mad at you," he said. "Besides, it does the rest of us good to see Miss Brain get something wrong once in a while."

Before I could reply, Maggie and Miss Rourke came back with two big branches. Chubby took them and pushed them into the snowman's shoulders. Then Belinda and her entourage arrived bearing the coal nuggets. Chubby hoisted me up on his shoulders to decorate the face. When I jumped down again, we all stood back to admire our work.

"Now, that's a snowman!" I declared.

"Still needs something," Chubby mumbled, crossing his arms and staring critically at the snowman.

"A hat!" said Maggie.

"Exactly," said Chubby. He gazed around at the crowd, then his eyes met mine and he smiled wickedly. I knew exactly what that smile meant.

"No you don't," I said, covering my hat with both hands and starting to run.

Chubby pounded after me across the green. He caught up with me on the bank of the millpond, hit me with a flying tackle, and we tumbled into the snow, laughing and shrieking as we rolled over and over each other down to the frozen pond. I landed on my back on the ice with Chubby on top of me. He pinned my hands up over my head with one hand and tried to snatch the hat with the other.

I twisted my head back and forth, pretending to fight. In truth, though, I wasn't fighting too hard. It was a curious sensation, feeling Chubby's body stretched out on top of mine. I went all tingly and breathless, and I kind of liked it, but I wasn't sure I should. I mean, well jeepers, we're best friends, Chubby and I. Best friends shouldn't make each other feel tingly. It just wasn't cricket. I let the pretend struggle go on for about as long as I thought prudent with Miss Rourke and the rest of the school watching. Then I pulled a hand free, grabbed a fistful of snow, and mashed it into Chubby's face. He rolled off, and I jumped up and sprinted back up the bank. In a flash he was after me with a snowball in his hand. I ran behind Miss Rourke just as he let it fly.

SPLAT! It hit her right dead center in the bust, clinging to her wool coat and sticking out like a third bosom.

Chubby froze.

Miss Rourke stood looking down at her chest for a stunned moment, then she laughed out loud, grabbed the third bosom, and hurled it back at Chubby. Next thing we knew, the whole school was involved in a full-scale snowball fight. Miss Rourke lasted about fifteen minutes, then she threw her hands up in surrender and went home to correct papers. Belinda didn't last much longer. She got snow down her neck and went home sniffling.

The rest of us continued on, chasing through the streets of town, giggling and laughing and pelting one another with snowball after snowball. The snow stuck to our hats and mittens and woolen coats until we looked like a bunch of fuzzy white chicks with ruddy, red faces.

At last the clock on the town hall bonged the half hour and we realized that it was four-thirty.

"Jeepers creepers!" cried Maggie. "I didn't even notice it was getting so late. Ma's gonna skin me alive!"

Instantly everyone scattered. Night fell early in Enfield in winter, and all of us were supposed to be home by dusk.

Chubby and I ran back to the schoolhouse to collect our books.

"It's going to be pretty dark by the time you get home," Chubby said. "Want me to walk you?"

"Course not," I said. "I'm not afraid of the dark."

"I didn't mean that," said Chubby. "I meant, so you don't get a lickin'."

I laughed. "I don't get lickin's anymore," I said. "Sometimes I wish I did, though. I think a lickin' might be easier than some of Gran's tongue-lashings."

"So you want me to walk you or not?" asked Chubby.

"Nah. I'll be okay. I'll walk fast. Maybe somebody will come by and give me a ride."

"Doubt it," said Chubby. "Not many cars out in this weather. I think you better let me walk you."

I looked at him and squinted my eyes teasingly. "I swear, Chubby Miller, you've got a nose like a hound dog. You can tell all the way from here that Gran baked a fresh apple pie this mornin', can't you?"

Chubby's eyes widened. "Well, not really," he said, "but now that you mention it. . . ." He licked his lips.

I laughed. "All right, come on," I said. "I'll get you an invite to supper."

3

When we got as far as Chubby's daddy's filling station, Chubby ran around back to tell his ma he wouldn't be home for dinner. I waited out front.

Mr. Howell came out to shovel the post office steps. He gave a shout when he saw me.

"Celie," he called. "Come on over here. Got a letter inside for your grandmother."

"Can't it wait till tomorrow, Mr. Howell?" I asked. "I'm kind of late."

"Won't take but a minute," he said, ducking back into the post office. I walked over, and Mrs. Walsh came out with her mail in her hand. I ran up the steps to help her down.

"Careful. It's very slippery," I said.

"Thank you, dear," she said, leaning on my arm as she labored down one stair tread at a time.

"How's Mr. Walsh doing?" I asked her. Old man Walsh had been suffering with the consumption for some time.

"Took a turn for the worse, I'm afraid," said Mrs. Walsh. "And this sure isn't goin' to help." She held up an opened letter.

"What is it?" I asked.

Mrs. Walsh patted my shoulder. "You'll see soon enough, dear," she said with a sigh, then she hobbled off down the street.

"Watch your step, now," I called after her.

Mr. Howell came out again and handed me an envelope. "Now, don't you lose it. It's important," he said.

I looked at the envelope suspiciously. "What's in it?" I asked.

"You'll find out soon enough," said Mr. Howell. "Just see to it that it gets home safely."

I stared at the return address on the letter—MDWSC. Those letters filled me with dread. They stood for Metropolitan District Water Supply Commission.

I looked back up at Mr. Howell. "It's from the commission," I said.

He nodded shortly. "That it is. Now run along. It's gettin' dark."

I was tempted to open the mysterious envelope right then and there. But it was addressed to Gran, and I knew she'd have my hide if I opened her mail. I tucked it into my pocket.

"Celie," someone called. "Celie Wheeler, come here a minute, love."

I turned to see Lydia Rogers poking her head out of her dry goods shop. I groaned to myself. Mrs. Rogers was the town busybody. From the way she was grinning, I was quite sure she had some juicy tidbit she wanted me to carry home to Mama and Gran.

"It's getting late, Mrs. Rogers," I said. "I'm supposed to be home b'fore dark."

"Oh." Mrs. Rogers looked crestfallen. Then she brightened. "Well, you tell your mother to stop by the shop for a cup of tea tomorrow, will you? I'm packing things up to move, and I have some dimity I think she might like."

"Yes, ma'am," I said quietly. "I'll do that."

Chubby came out of the filling station.

"You ready?" he asked.

I nodded and hurried after him before any more well-meaning neighbors could waylay me.

4

"Celie? Cecelia, is that you?" Mama called through the door as Chubby and I paused on the back porch and stomped the snow from our boots.

"Yes, ma'am," I shouted. I pulled off my hat and smacked it against the wall to shake the snow loose, then I pushed through the door into the back hall. Chubby followed a step behind.

The kitchen beyond was bathed in golden light. Mama stood by the stove in her faded blue housedress, stirring something in our black enamel soup kettle. Chicken-scented steam bubbled up and drifted in wispy clouds around the bare lightbulb over her head.

"It's quite dark, Cecelia," she said, brushing back a damp strand of yellow hair. "I was starting to worry."

"Sorry," I said, plopping my books on the deacon's bench in the hall and tugging at my boots. "I brought Chubby home for supper. I hope that's all right. We were building a snowman, and then we all got into a snowball fight. I guess we lost track of the time. Then it seemed like everyone in town had *something* to say to me on the way home."

"Chubby, you're always welcome," Mama said with a smile, "but . . . won't your folks worry about you walking home so late in this storm?"

"My daddy's goin' out plowing after supper," Chubby said. "He's going to swing by and pick me up around eight."

Mama nodded. "All right then," she said.

Chubby and I pulled off our coats and tossed them over empty hooks by the door.

Mama smiled again as we walked into the kitchen. "My goodness, Randall," she said to Chubby. "You grow another inch every time I see you. Celie, don't you think it's time we started calling Randall by his given name? There isn't anything chubby about him now, the way he's sprung up."

I looked at Chubby. "How about it, *Randall*?" I said.

He grimaced and I laughed. He knew I could no more call him Randall than I could call Mama, Helen, or Gran, Lizzie.

"He'll always be Chubby to me," I told Mama, "no matter how tall and skinny he gets."

"I don't mind, Mrs. Wheeler," said Chubby. He sniffed the air and turned toward Gran's fresh-baked apple pie. "I still feel like Chubby on the inside."

Mama chuckled and turned back to the stove. "Well, long as you don't mind, I don't suppose it does any harm." She grabbed an onion out of the basket over her head and started peeling it. "How was school today?"

"Okay," I said. "Sure was hard to keep my mind on my books, though, with all that snow. Which reminds me—I came up with a new simile!"

"Oh?" said Mama.

I reached my arms out toward the window, where the falling snow glittered in the beam of the back porch light.

"Like dandruff shook loose from God's head," I said dramatically.

Mama's eyes widened and her lips twitched. She gave a little cough.

"What?" I said. "Don't you like it?"

"Oh, yes," she said. "It's . . . very descriptive."

I grinned and walked over to give her a quick kiss, then Chubby and I shook out our snow-crusted mittens in the old, gray soapstone laundry sink and put them on the warming rack over the stove to dry. They soon started to steam, and the smell of wet wool mingled with the buttery scent of Mama's chicken soup.

Ginger came running from the dining room and rubbed herself against my ankles. I picked her up and gave her a kiss on the tip of her nose. She sneezed one of her little kitten sneezes and shook her head.

"What did you learn today?" Mama asked.

Chubby chortled. "She learned where Madagascar is," he quipped.

I looked at him and my eyes narrowed.

"Which reminds me of a little unfinished business," I said. I put Ginger down and started wiggling my fingers. Chubby had one weakness. He was ticklish.

"Oh no," he said. "No you don't."

"Oh, yes I do," I warned.

Chubby ran around the kitchen table. I ran after him. He ran around again, trying to keep the table between us.

"Now, Celie," said Mama.

"Stop her, Mrs. Wheeler," Chubby pleaded.

I started around one way, then quick doubled back. Chubby tried to turn, too, but he wasn't fast enough. I lunged and grabbed him by the shirt. With the other hand I went to work.

"Ah! Eeeeee!" Chubby screamed, writhing like a worm on a fishhook.

"Mrs. Wheeler!" he cried again, then he broke loose and ran into the dining room.

I tore after him.

"Celie! Stop that! You're going to break something!" Mama shouted.

Chubby raced through the dining room and out into the hall. He ran in through one end of the parlor and out the other, then down the hall and around again. I changed direction in the hall and met him in the middle of the parlor. He tried to turn, but I leaped onto his shoulders and pulled him down onto the carpet. I climbed on his back, yanked up his shirt and started in on his bare middle with both hands—fingers wiggling like . . . like Medusa's hair.

"Please. No. Help!" Chubby gasped, laughing and thrashing. I was laughing so hard I could hardly catch my breath, either. He was trying to buck me off like a bronco.

"Land sakes!" someone shouted.

We both paused, breathing hard, and looked up.

There stood Gran, her starched cotton apron tied neatly about the waist of her navy blue flowered dress, her white hair pulled back smoothly in its customary bun, not a strand out of place. She frowned.

"What *are* you doing, Cecelia?" she demanded.

"Ti . . . tickling," I said, when I could catch my breath.

She shook her head. "Aren't you getting a bit old to be rolling around on the floor like a common ragamuffin?"

"I agree completely, Mrs. Wheeler," Chubby wheezed, "This is . . . no way for a young lady. . . ."

"Stow it, Miller," I said. Then I pushed my mussed hair back from my face and climbed off of him.

"I'm not too old," I told Gran. "I'm only fourteen." Then I grinned. "Besides, I fully intend to keep rolling around on the floor till I'm old as you are, Gran."

A little smile tugged at Gran's lip. "Well, won't that be a sight," she said.

I giggled.

5

"Come along now," said Gran. "If the two of you have so much energy to spare, I'd best put you to work."

Chubby and I groaned, then got up and followed her out to the kitchen.

"Celie, you set the table," said Gran. "Chubby, you go on out to the carriage house and bring in some more firewood."

"Yes, ma'am," said Chubby, heading for the back hall.

I got the dishes from the cupboard and started putting them on the table.

"By the way, I saw Mrs. Walsh downtown," I told Gran. "She says Hiram's feeling poorly again."

"Oh dear." Gran clicked her tongue. "I'll have to stop by and bring him some soup."

"Oh, and Mama," I added, "Mrs. Rogers said to tell you to stop in for tea tomorrow. She's got some dimity she wants to show you."

Mama laughed. "More likely she's picked up some juicy tidbit of gossip she's dying to share."

Gran nodded. "That woman does love carrying tales. She's harmless, though, for the most part."

Chubby came back in with an armload of wood and set it down by the stove.

"You want me to put in some more, Mrs. Wheeler?" he asked.

"Not right now, thank you," said Gran.

Knock, knock, knock went Mama's knife on the cutting board, dicing the onion into fine bits. "Celie, did you check for mail?" she asked.

"Oh, *yes!*" I cried, suddenly remembering. I ducked back into the hall and pulled the damp envelope from my coat pocket. "It's for you, Gran," I said. "Mr. Howell down to the post office said it's important."

Gran walked into the center of the kitchen, the faint scent of lavender wafting about her like a fresh breeze in the stuffy room. She took the envelope from my hand, held it at arm's length, and squinted at the return address.

"Danged water commission again," she grumbled. "What d'they want now?"

Chubby and I exchanged apprehensive glances as Gran fumbled with the envelope. Once she got the letter free, Gran took her reading glasses from her apron pocket and perched them on her nose. Her lips moved and she mumbled under her breath as she worked her way down the page. When she reached the end, she snorted and threw the letter down on the table.

"What is it?" Mama asked.

"Horsefeathers," Gran replied.

Mama wiped her hands on her apron, then dabbed at her eyes, teary from the onion. She picked up the letter.

"What does it say?" I asked, peering anxiously over her shoulder.

"Says it's time to go," Mama answered quietly. "They want us all out by April first."

My throat tightened. "Out . . ." I croaked. "What do you mean, *out*?"

"Out of our houses. Out of town," Mama said, looking at me solemnly, "so they can start the flooding."

"*The flooding*," rasped Chubby.

The words smacked into my chest like a medicine ball. "But . . ." Chubby and I exchanged troubled glances. "We won't even be done with school by April first," I said.

Mama sniffed and dabbed at her eyes again. I examined her face to see if the tears were real this time. "Darn onion," she mumbled.

Gran folded her arms across her chest. "Don't you worry none, Cecelia," she said. "We aren't goin' anywhere."

Mama sighed. "Gran," she said, "this looks pretty official to me."

"Official, my foot," snapped Gran. She took the letter from Mama's hand and crumpled it, then she opened the stove door and tossed it in.

"Go ahead and set the table for supper, Cecelia," she said, "and don't pay no nevermind to that letter. You young folks have gone to school right here in Enfield all eight grades, and by golly you're going to have your graduation come June jest like you deserve."

"Gran," said Mama pointedly, "you can't be makin' promises that—"

"'Nough said," Gran snapped. She turned on her heel and stomped into the pantry.

Chubby and I stood staring at the stove door, watching the flare of the burning letter. *Someday* had suddenly become starkly, terribly real. This town we loved, everything we knew, the very roads we walked on, would soon rest beneath the waters of a giant reservoir, like some scene in a dimestore waterglobe. What would become of us, of me and Chubby, and Mama and Gran? And what about all our friends and neighbors? Who would we be without Enfield to bind us together?

"Celie," Mama said firmly.

I looked at her.

"I believe you were asked to set the table."

6

Supper was awkwardly quiet. Chubby and I were brim-ful of qualms and questions, but Gran wouldn't tolerate any discussion. We tried, but the reservoir was a closed sub-ject. The letter had never come as far as Gran was concerned, an attitude that seemed to irk Mama to no end. The tension between the two of them was like a twisted wire, ready to snap.

Outside, the wind was rising. It rattled the loose shutter on the porch and groaned in the eaves of the portico. The bare branches of the lilac bush scratched at the kitchen win-dow, like a cat begging to come in.

"Gotta cut that bush back come spring," said Gran.

Mama sighed noisily, irritation radiating from her body like heat from the stove. Chubby looked at me with raised eyebrows.

"Want some pie?" I asked him.

He shrugged. "Sure, I guess."

"How 'bout you, Mama?"

"I'm not hungry," Mama said shortly.

"Gran?" I asked.

"Hot as tarnation in here," Gran grumbled by way of reply. "I'm goin' out for a breath of air."

"It's mighty cold out there, Mrs. Wheeler," said Chubby.

"Not goin' far," Gran mumbled.

"Chubby and I will go with you," I offered.

"Don't you have homework?" snapped Mama.

Gran's eyes flickered in Mama's direction.

"Yes," I said, "but I . . ."

"You children do yer homework," Gran said quietly, then she shuffled into the hall, put on her coat and boots, and tied a scarf around her head. The door jingled as it banged shut behind her, and Ginger went bounding out to swat at the old harness bells that dangled from the latch.

Mama stared after Gran a long moment, then sighed heavily.

"Why are you so angry with Gran?" I asked.

Mama shook her head. "I'm not," she said tiredly. "It's just . . . I think it's time she faced facts."

"You think they mean what they say in that letter?" Chubby asked.

"Oh, they mean it." Mama nodded.

"April first?" My throat tightened as I ticked off the days in my mind. "That's less than two months away," I said. "How can they throw us out so fast?"

"So fast?" Mama looked at me in surprise. "Come on Celie. We've known this was coming for ten years—ever since they passed the Swift River Act back in 'twenty-eight.

And there were rumors long before that. You can't tell me you haven't noticed everyone moving out and all the shops closing up downtown."

"I know," I said, "but . . . I guess I just didn't think the end would ever *really* come."

Chubby nodded slowly. "Me neither," he said.

I cut two pieces of pie and carried them over to the table for Chubby and me. We ate in silence while Mama started washing up the supper dishes.

I thought back over the years, about all the warning signs I'd chosen to ignore. The two dams were the biggest, of course. They had risen up out of the earth like giant mole-hills, creeping along to seal off the end of the valley and turn it into a big bowl. But the construction had been so much a part of our lives that it had just sort of faded into the scenery. It was easy to forget what the dams were and why they were being built. Sitting on the hillsides and watching the great earth machines at work was just another valley pastime, like following behind the plows, searching for arrowheads, or rolling old tires up and down the hills. The hum and clank of machinery in the distance was so constant that on Sundays, when all was quiet, it seemed like something was missing.

It was true that a lot of our valley friends had moved away. It hadn't been as bad in Enfield as in the other towns, though. Most of our neighbors did sell out in the early 1930s, but a lot of them had stayed on, renting their farms and houses back from the commission, and they still lived in them, just like always.

There were plenty of kids around, too, because lots of new kids had moved into town over the years. Some came because the Depression took their fathers' jobs, and the commission was renting out the vacant farms and land really cheap. For five dollars a month folks could get a house, barns, and enough acreage to grow their own food. Lots of families had been getting through the Depression that way.

Others came because their fathers were hired on to the project. More stores and businesses opened up to serve all the new people, too, so up until the last year or so, Enfield had been livelier than ever. Which made it all the harder to believe that *someday* was actually coming.

I looked over at Chubby. "I guess maybe I didn't think about it on purpose," I said. "It seemed like, maybe if I didn't think about it, it would go away."

Mama lifted her apron over her head. "I know that feeling, Celie," she said gently, "but it doesn't work. You can't bury your troubles under a rock. Sooner or later they always manage to work their way back above ground."

"But the commission *has* to let us stay until we graduate," Chubby insisted. "It wouldn't be fair to split us up and make us graduate from other schools when June is just a few months away."

Mama smiled. "Well," she said, "Gran's an old blueblood. She's still got a lot of clout in this town. If I were you, I wouldn't start packing my bags just yet." She gave us a wink.

"Blueblood" is what they called folks who'd lived in the valley forever. One of Gran's ancestors, Jedediah Crocker, was given land in the valley back in the early 1700s because he fought the Indians in King Philip's War, and Gran's family had owned the land ever since. When Gran was young, her daddy was a big man in Enfield—a mill owner and a gentleman farmer. She was rich then. We weren't rich anymore by the time I was born. We managed okay, though. There was always food on the table and fuel for the furnace and stove, and if our clothes were a bit tattered, well . . . with the Depression on, whose weren't? I never was really sure what we lived on. Neither Mama nor Gran ever worked for pay that I can recall. Gran put up vegetables from her garden and had a shelf down at Haskell's General Store, and Mama peddled homemade pies and baked beans to the lake folk in the summer, but I know that wasn't enough to get us by. I figured the money must have come from selling off the land, and maybe from Grandfather's and Daddy's insurances.

My father and grandfather both died young. Heart, you know. Gran always was fond of saying that the Wheeler men were just too kindhearted for the meanness of this world. I never knew my grandfather, and I don't much remember my daddy, either. I was only two when he died. I feel like I know him, though, from pictures and things we've always had around, and from all the stories Mama and Gran have told me about him. He loved Enfield and the valley, and I'm glad he didn't have to see it dying.

Mama hung her apron on its hook beside the sink. She came over to the table and offered us another piece of pie. Chubby took one, but I was full.

Mama looked at the half a pie that was left.

"You know," she said, "I think I'll take the rest of this on up to the Clarks. Sue stopped by to borrow an egg today, and it pained me to see how scrawny those little boys of hers are. I gave them each a couple of cookies, and I wish you could see how they relished them!"

I smiled. "That would be nice, Mama," I said.

The Clarks were our nearest neighbors—the nearest ones that were left anyway. They were renting one of the abandoned houses, but Mr. Clark had been out of work since '33 and it was a struggle for them to pay even the five dollars a month rent sometimes.

Mama wrapped up the pie in a newspaper and put on her coat and boots. "You two better get a start on your homework," she said. "If you need any help, I'll be back soon."

I nodded, but after Mama left, I just sat, listening to the familiar sounds of the house around me while Chubby finished his pie; the crackling of the wood in the stove, the ticking of the grandfather clock in the front hall, the hissing and banging of the old steam radiators—sounds as comforting as an old quilt. It was hard to keep tears from my eyes.

"How can they take our houses away from us?" I said out loud. "They're like a part of us."

I didn't really expect an answer. There was none, and Chubby knew it. He just went on chewing quietly.

Ginger was asleep on the windowsill between a couple of potted plants, her fuzzy little pink belly rising and falling with each breath. I got up and went over and picked her up, wiping my damp eyes on her fur. She pulled back and batted my nose with her paws.

"It's not fair, is it, Ginger?" I asked.

Ginger was annoyed at being awakened and in no mood to console me. She leapt from my arms to the floor, then skittered off sideways, chasing one of those little demons that only kittens seem to see.

I sighed heavily and went out into the hall to pick up my

books. Chubby came and got his, too, and we spread them across the kitchen table.

"We're going to need a dictionary, and an atlas, too," said Chubby.

I nodded. "They're up in my room," I said. "I'll get them."

I started through the dining room, then stopped, looking around fondly at the old house, the graceful high ceilings and tall windows, the beautiful mantelpiece. . . .

It was still a fine house, I thought, even if it *was* run-down. It had eighteen rooms, though most of them hadn't been used in years. Many of them were servants' quarters on the third floor. Chubby and I had always loved playing up there, so many keen little nooks and crannies, so many great places to hide.

There hadn't been any servants in the house since the turn of the century, when Gran's daddy's mill failed. She and my grandfather had struggled hard to keep the farm, working it themselves after that. The closest thing we ever had to a servant in my lifetime was our farmhand, Cal, who Gran hired after my grandfather died. But Cal had "moved on" years ago, and we'd been making due ourselves ever since. Mama had suggested to Gran from time to time that we ought to make use of all our empty rooms by taking in boarders, but Gran would never hear of it. She said her mother would roll over in her grave at the thought of her lovely home being turned into a common rooming house.

So we'd kept the house up as best we could, but every year it got a bit saggier, and a little grayer. "Just like me," Gran was fond of saying. "She may be showing her age a bit on the outside, but she's still sound as a dollar on the inside, and that's where it counts."

The house was built high atop Great Quabbin Hill to afford a commanding view of the valley from its white-pillared porch. A long driveway curved up from the street, passed under the portico on the right side of the house, then proceeded on to the carriage house and the barns out back. Stone walls lined the drive, and here and there ancient oaks and maples leaned over them with their great heads close together, reminding me of neighbors whispering secrets.

I feel lucky to have grown up in such a house. Why, we even had indoor plumbing and electric lights. We'd had a telephone for a while, too, but Gran said the ringing was an annoyance. I think, in truth, we couldn't keep up the bills. We'd done fine without, though. Not many Enfield folks could boast such modern conveniences, mostly just those that lived downtown. Downtown. Mama always laughed to hear me call Enfield downtown. She said it never was much more than a whistle-stop on the old Rabbit Train run from Athol to Springfield. And for years now even the train had been gone.

"Hey."

I turned. Chubby was standing in the dining room doorway.

"You get lost?" he asked.

I smiled. "Sorry. Just daydreaming, I guess."

"Well, come on," he said, pushing past me up the stairs. "Let's get those books. I want to get started."

I followed him, fitting my feet into the worn depressions on the marble treads as I climbed. My hand slid slowly up the banister, rubbed shiny and smooth by the hands of my ancestors. Some of their pictures smiled down at me from the wall.

Chubby paused at the door to my room and looked back at me. "Now what are you doing?" he asked.

"Looking at the pictures," I said.

Chubby shook his head. "Why? It's not like you've never seen them before."

I just shrugged.

Chubby took a step back and looked at the pictures too. "I don't think I ever really noticed them," he said. "Who are they?"

I pointed. "That's my father," I said, "and this is my grandfather."

"Is that you?" asked Chubby, pointing to a photograph of a little girl. A small bronze plaque on the frame bore the name CECELIA.

"No," I said. "That's my aunt, my father's little sister. I'm named for her. She died when she was only three."

Chubby shook his head. "Jeepers," he said, "your grandmother's had a rough life, huh?"

I nodded. "Yeah," I said, "and now they want to take her home away."

Chubby pointed to the last two portraits.

"Who are *they*?" he asked.

"My great-grandparents."

"Were they as mean as they look?"

I laughed. "No, they just look like that because it was such a pain to get your picture taken back then. You couldn't move a muscle or everything would blur."

"Still, they could have smiled," said Chubby.

I shrugged. "I suppose. Gran says her father was actually pretty jolly—even a little *too* jolly sometimes."

"What do you mean?" asked Chubby.

I giggled. "Well, he used to go into town in the evening now and then, to business meetings, supposedly. Then sometime in the night, long after Gran was in bed, she'd wake up and hear singing in the distance—or bellowing, more like it, she said. Sure enough, before long there'd come the *clip-clop* of hooves, bringing her daddy's buggy up the drive. Next thing, she'd hear him stumbling on the hall stairs. Sometimes he'd start singing again and she'd hear her mother shushing him. 'Hush now, before Lizzie hears,' she'd say." I laughed. "As if anyone could sleep with all that racket."

Chubby laughed, too, and continued to stare at my great-grandmother's portrait.

"She sure doesn't look the type to put up with much tom-foolery," he said.

I shrugged. "Well, she could be stern at times, I guess. Gran said she had to be. She was the one that really ran things—the house, the farm. She even kept the books for the business. Gran says she was smart as a whip."

Chubby looked at me. "So that's where the Wheeler brains come from?" he asked.

I smiled. "Could be. Gran says her mother loved a good time as much as anyone, though. They used to throw lavish parties here in the old days."

Chubby nodded. "I've heard," he said. "My grandmother used to tell stories about coming to parties here when she was a little girl."

I sighed. "Can't you just picture it?" I said dreamily. "Like a Hollywood movie, with carriages pulling up to the portico and dropping off their passengers, the women all dressed in elegant gowns, the men in top hats and tails. . . . Don't you wish you could have seen it back then?"

"Yeah." Chubby looked around. "I'll bet the old place was really somethin' in its day."

"Yes," I said, "and Gran was too." I dragged Chubby down the hall to show him another portrait—Gran, in her wedding gown, with her lovely lace train pooled around her feet. Her dark eyes glowed, and her shining auburn hair fell in soft curls over her shoulders.

"Wow," he said, "she was a looker."

"The wedding was held here," I said. "I had always hoped mine would be too." Then I sighed and stared at the threadbare carpet that ran the length of the upstairs hall and at the yellowed, peeling paper on the walls.

"I wonder what my great-grandmother would think of her beautiful house now," I said softly. "I wonder how she'd feel if she knew. . . ." My voice cracked, and I could feel tears stinging my nose.

"Hey," said Chubby gently, "don't think about that, okay? Don't make it worse than it is."

I nodded slowly and cleared my throat. "You're right," I said. "C'mon. Let's go get those books."

Chubby followed me into my room and stood staring at all the Bing Crosby and Clark Gable pictures I had plastered all over my walls.

"You must have a thing for ears," he teased.

"Hey," I said, "if you had dimples like Clark or a voice like Bing, I'd have a thing for you too. I wouldn't care if you had elephant ears."

"Bubba bubba boo-o-o," Chubby crooned.

"Oh please," I said, sticking my fingers in my ears.

A movement outside caught my eye. I walked to the window and rubbed a little clear spot in the frosty pane.

"What is it?" asked Chubby.

"It's Gran," I said.

He walked over and rubbed the spot larger. Below us on the lawn stood Gran, all alone in the dark, snow swirling around her as she stared silently down upon the warm, familiar lights of the valley.

"Poor Gran," I whispered hoarsely.

Chubby put an arm around my shoulder and squeezed.

7

The April 1 deadline came and went, and we stayed on. Gran had mustered a group of citizens to speak out at the town meeting back in February about how the town's children should be allowed to finish out the school year, and as usual, she got her way. Lots of folks didn't stay, though. After those notices went out, people started leaving in droves. Only a handful of kids were left in school now—the eighth graders who were staying to graduate, and a few others. Most everyone was planning to leave right after school ended, except for Chubby and his family. The MDWSC needed fuel for its vehicles, so Chubby and his folks would stay on and run the filling station until the bitter end.

I couldn't ignore *someday* anymore, though. Extra teams had come in to cut trees and brush and tear down buildings, and the valley had started disappearing before my very eyes. Trucks went by every day, hauling out lumber from the torn-down homes and barns. Moving trucks and cars piled high with furniture and personal belongings rumbled past. Farmers herded their sheep and cattle right down the center of the road on their way to distant pastures. My stomach sank whenever I saw a favorite tree fall, or a friend's house crumble beneath the wreckers' hammers. Sometimes it felt like I was witnessing the coming of doomsday.

It got harder and harder to pay attention in school, what with buildings getting torn down all around us, and shopkeepers closing up and moving out left and right. Lots of days Miss Rourke would just give up and let us talk about the valley and what we were feeling.

Despite everything, though, Gran still had her heels dug in. We were halfway through April and she hadn't sold out yet. Whenever anybody asked when she was going to move, she'd just shake her head and say, "When the water comes up to m'doorstep." That was just her way of being stubborn, because in truth the water never would get to our doorstep. We lived in what was to be the watershed area, which was a big part of why Gran couldn't understand us being put out. The commission said that everybody and everything that might contaminate the water had to go, and that included us, but Gran said she'd never contaminated anything in her life, and the commission probably did more contaminating with all their trucks and machines than the whole rest of us put together.

Charlie Parker came by a lot. He was a neighbor and an old friend of Gran's, but he'd been hired by the MDWSC to try to get people to sell. He tried just about every approach in the book with Gran, but he always left scratching his head.

"You can't go on pretending it isn't going to happen," Mama would complain impatiently after each of Charlie's visits. "The dams are near done. They'll be letting the water go any day now."

Gran just stood there ramrod straight with those arms of hers crossed over her heart like an iron gate. "You can go any time you want," she'd snap at Mama. "Nobody's stoppin' ya."

Then Mama would sigh in frustration. "You know we're not going to leave you," she'd say. And that would be the end of it—until Charlie Parker came around again.

I had a feeling they were going to have to carry Gran out of that house, kicking and scrapping every step of the way.

"What a beautiful spring day," Mama said at dinner one Saturday toward the end of April. "You should get outside, Celie. I'm surprised Chubby hasn't shown up yet."

"He's helpin' his daddy out down to the station today," I said.

"Just as well," said Gran. "Seems to my mind that you and that young man are spending an unnatural amount of time together of late."

My mouth fell open. "Unnatural," I said. "What's unnatural about me and Chubby being together?"

"He's a boy and you're a girl," said Gran. "Girls ought to have other girls for friends, if you ask me."

"There *are* no other girls since the Kramer twins moved away," I said.

"There's the Wilder girl," said Gran.

I made a face like I was gagging. "That priss-face," I said. "I'd be bored to tears palling around with her."

"Might do you good," said Gran. "You could do with a bit more priss."

Mama laughed. "Celie and Chubby have been best friends since they were babies, Gran," she said. "I don't see any harm in it."

"The harm in it is, they're *not* babies anymore," said Gran. "They're of that age."

"What age?" I asked.

"The age when boys don't have but one thing on their minds," said Gran.

"What?" I asked.

"Sparkin'," said Gran.

I burst out laughing. "Chubby's not like that," I said.

Gran wagged a finger at me. "You heed my words," she insisted. "All teenaged boys are like that. Can't help themselves. They're just like bulls in springtime, even when it isn't springtime a'tal."

"But it *is* springtime," I said.

"All the worse," said Gran.

Mama smiled. "Celie and Chubby only have a couple of months left to spend time together, Gran," she said. "Let them be."

My heart lurched at Mama's words. Somehow I had always assumed that, no matter where I ended up, Chubby would be there too.

"But . . . don't you think maybe we'll move to the same town as Chubby?" I asked.

Gran's face closed up the way it always did whenever anyone mentioned moving, and Mama gave me a "we'll discuss that later" look. Then she changed the subject.

"I'm walking into town to get the mail and pick up a few things at Haskell's," she said. "Would you like to join me, Celie?"

"No," I said. "I think I'll just stay here and read. I want to finish *Gone with the Wind*."

"Finish?" said Mama. "I thought Aunt Stella just loaned you that book a few days ago."

"She did, but I can't put it down. It's the *berries*, Ma. You've got to read it. You too, Gran. It's got all kinds of history in it."

"And a little romance, from what I hear," Mama added with a wink.

I smiled. "A little," I admitted, then hugged my arms to my chest. "I heard on the radio that Clark Gable is going to play Rhett Butler in the movie. It's coming out next year. Can we go see it right away, Mama?"

Mama shrugged. "Well, that'll depend on where we're living, I guess," she said with a cautious glance in Gran's direction.

Gran pretended not to hear.

"It will be a long time before a movie like that gets to Ware or Amherst," Mama continued.

I huffed. "Well, can we go into Springfield, then? I'll just die if I don't get to see it right away. Everyone will be talking about it."

Gran snorted. "Be a cold day in August b'fore anybody in this family treks all the way to Springfield just to see some fool movie," she said.

"But Gran," I pleaded. "It's not *just* a movie. It's Clark Gable!"

I hadn't seen many movies in my life—just a handful at most, but one of them was *It Happened One Night* with Clark Gable and Claudette Colbert, and I've been in love with Clark Gable ever since.

"Gabel Schmabel," said Gran.

Mama chuckled. "Next year's a long way off," she said. "No sense in arguing any more about this right now."

"All right," I said with a sigh, "but I just have to see it somehow. Clark will just be the dreamiest, I know. I keep picturing him in the part as I'm reading."

"And just who are you picturing as Miss Scarlett?" asked Mama with a merry chuckle.

I blushed and grinned.

Gran clucked her tongue.

"You mind my words, Helen," she said to Mama. "She's too young to have her head filled with all that stuff and nonsense."

Mama laughed. "Oh, come now, Gran," she said. "You can't tell me you didn't enjoy a good romantic tale when you were Celie's age. I'll bet *Wuthering Heights* had you swooning over Heathcliff."

Gran sniffed. "Never *swooned* in my life," she said, then her lips twitched and the corners curled upward. "We called it *getting the vapors*," she added.

Mama and I laughed, and finally Gran joined in.

"Well, I'm not going to try to compete with Clark Gable," said Mama. "I guess I'll be walking to town alone. That is, unless you're in the mood for a little fresh air, Gran?"

Gran shook her head. "Mouthful'a dust is more like it," she said. "No, you go ahead, Helen. All them big machines down there hurt my ears. Besides, it disheartens me to see what they're doin' to the town."

"All right," Mama said as she headed out the door with her purse over her arm. "I won't be long."

"Take your time," Gran called after her. "Nothin' doin' here."

I offered to help Gran with the dishes, but she shooed me outside.

"Take that book of yours out on the porch," she said. "It's far too fine a day to be wastin' indoors."

"Thanks, Gran," I said, then I grabbed up *Gone with the Wind* and skeedaddled outside before she changed her mind and found some other chore that needed doing.

It *was* nice out, one of those spring-fever days that teased you into thinking summer had already arrived. The breeze was soft as pussy willow down and sweet as milk warm from the cow. A chickadee darted back and forth from a nearby tree, investigating all the nooks and crannies of the porch ceiling, deciding where to build her nest. With a stab of sorrow I realized that she might not be safe there. What if the wreckers came before her nestlings had fledged? Sadly, I chased her away. "Not here, little mother," I told her softly. "Not here."

In the distance, I could hear the ever-present rumble of the giant earthmovers. The sound brought home Mama's words. *Celie and Chubby only have a couple of months. . . . "*

A heavy weight seemed to settle on my chest. What would life be like without Chubby to laugh and tease with, to share secrets and sorrows with? I could find other friends, sure, but would they know my mind and my moods the way Chubby did? Would they know when I needed cheering and when I just needed company? It was plain too hard to think about. Mama said you couldn't put your troubles under a rock, but maybe we *would* end up living in the same town as Chubby. It was certainly possible. I buried my worries deep, hoping that just this once the rock would stay put.

I curled up on the front porch swing and started to turn

the pages, slipping away from the sorrows of my world and into the adventures of Scarlett O'Hara's. Ginger scampered through last year's moldy leaves for a while, chasing squirrels and chipmunks, then she hopped up on my lap, kneaded my skirt into a little nest, and snuggled down for a nap. An hour passed, maybe more, and the gentle swaying of the swing and the warmth of the sun made me drowsy. My eyelids drooped and drooped, until at last I closed my book and drifted off to sleep.

8

An extra loud rumble woke me from my nap and I opened my eyes to see a small house going by, all in one piece, on a flatbed truck. I stared at it jealously. It may not have been much of a house, but to someone it was home, and they were getting to keep it. I wished we could afford to have our house moved. Why did it have to be so big? Why did we have to be so poor?

Suddenly a flash of color caught my eye. There was a canary yellow convertible making its way up the hill from town. I stared as it came closer. I'd never seen such a keen car! It didn't belong to anybody in Enfield, that was for sure. At first I figured it must be another sightseer. We'd had lots of those lately—come to gawk at the valley and the dams, and at us, like we were some sort of circus freak show. The car kept coming though and, to my amazement, turned in at our driveway! I jumped up and ran over to it.

"Leapin' lizards, mister," I said, leaning over the driver's door to peer at the fancy dashboard. "This is some jalopy!"

The man chuckled. "You like it?" he asked.

"Like it!" I cried. "It's the *berries*! What is it?"

"It's a British car. They call it an MG."

"Jeepers," I responded. "Say! Maybe you could take me for a drive sometime?"

The man laughed. "You're not shy, are you?"

"Nope," I said, then I looked at him for the first time. Whoa, was he handsome! I mean, he made Clark Gable look like . . . like a big cow plop!

"Wow," I said out loud.

"Wow what?" he asked.

"Um . . . Wow, you are, um . . . not very old to have a car like this."

He smiled and I nearly swooned. Two adorable, Clark Gable-like dimples appeared just above the corners of his mouth. "I'm twenty-four," he said, "and I guess that must be old enough because, as you can see, I've got it."

"And how," I said dreamily.

His eyes were blue. Deep blue. Like the bluing Mama and Gran always mixed in with the whites on laundry day.

He laughed and shook his head and a few silky strands of corn silk hair tumbled down over one eye. "Allow me to introduce myself," he said, offering his hand. "Name's Jacob Taylor."

"Charmed, I'm sure," I said, grabbing his hand and squeezing it tight.

"Would you . . . um . . . mind letting me out of my car?"

"Oh." I dropped his hand and jumped back. "Sorry."

"No problem." He picked his fedora up off the passenger seat, perched it on the back of his beautiful golden head, and climbed out of the car. He was tall and not too thin, not too fat—just right. He was a nifty dresser, too—had on a pin-striped suit with a navy blue tie, and those swell black and white shoes that were all the rage. Hotsy totsy, I thought to myself.

"Would your grandmother be at home?" he asked.

"Sure," I said, "why?"

Jacob Taylor gave me another one of his heart-fluttering smiles. "I'm here on business," he said. "I'm with the MDWSC."

"Oh," I said. My fluttering heart came in for a crash-landing. "Oh dear."

Jacob Taylor laughed. "That bad, huh?"

"Oh no," I said, trying not to be rude. "It's just that my grandmother . . . well, she . . ."

"Would rather speak to the devil himself?" He winked, and I started to laugh.

"I'm afraid that's about the size of it, Mr. Taylor."

He nodded. "I've been warned to expect as much." Then he straightened and looked around. His smile faded. "Can't say as I blame her. Mighty nice spot you've got here."

I looked around, too, seeing the graceful old house and grounds anew through the eyes of this stranger.

"Yes," I quietly agreed. "It is."

Jacob Taylor looked back at me and sighed. "I can't change things, though," he said. "I would if I could."

I nodded. "I know. It's not your fault, Mr. Taylor. Come on. My grandmother is inside."

"Hey," he said with a wink, "Mr. Taylor sounds like my father. Just call me Jake, okay?"

I blinked in surprise. "Oh, I couldn't," I said. "That is—I'm not allowed to call grown-ups by anything but their formal names."

"Grown-ups?" Jacob Taylor winced. "Come on. I'm not *that* much older than you, am I?"

I grinned in delight. "Why no," I said. "I suppose not."

"Good," he said. "Then it's Jake, okay? And you are?"

"Cecelia. Cecelia Wheeler, but . . . you can call me Celie if you like, only. . . ."

"Only what?"

"Only . . . maybe not in front of my grandmother."

Jake winked. "Gotcha," he said.

We walked beneath the portico, around to the back porch, and into the kitchen, where Gran was ironing linens. The kitchen smelled of steam and starch.

"We've got company, Gran," I said. "This is . . . um, Mr. Taylor. He's with the MDWSC."

Jake took his hat off and put out his hand. Gran looked over her shoulder at him, ignoring his outstretched hand, then she turned and fixed me with a stare. If her eyes could have shot bullets, I'd have been dead.

"Please don't blame your granddaughter, Mrs. Wheeler," Jake told her. "She tried to discourage me, but I persisted."

Gran turned back to her ironing. "Well, you can persist yerself right back out the door," she said, "b'cause I haven't anythin' to say to you."

"Mrs. Wheeler," said Jake, "I've been sent out here from the Boston office to help tie up loose ends and close out the relocation project. I've already been to see Doc Seaver and Mr. Peters. Thought you'd like to know they've both agreed to sell. You're about the only one left."

Gran put her flatiron back on the stove and turned around. "That don't make no nevermind to me," she said.

Jake fingered his hat brim impatiently. "Mrs. Wheeler," he said, "I understand how you feel, but—"

"*Don't* you tell me that!" snapped Gran, her eyes smoldering. She shook a finger in Jacob Taylor's face. "Don't you *dare* tell me you understand, young man. Is anybody takin' yer home away? Is anybody tellin' you to get off the land your people have farmed for two hunert years?"

"No," Jake admitted, "but if you'll just listen to reason."

"Reason?" Gran snorted. "*Reason?* Is it reasonable to take a body's home out from under 'em? I was born in this town, Mr. Taylor, and I birthed my babies in this very house. And both of them died here—one of a fever at the age of three, the other of a weak heart at twenty-seven." She paused and drew a long breath. "And come Monday . . . ," she added bitterly, "come Monday, do you know what I've got to *do*, Mr. Taylor?"

"No, ma'am," said Jake quietly.

"I've got to watch the MDWSC dig up their graves. Dig up my babies, just like they already dug up my husband, my mama and daddy, their mamas and daddies, and all the other Wheelers and Crockers that were laid to rest in this peaceful valley, thinkin' they were home for all time. Do you know how *that* feels, Mr. Taylor?"

Jake stood with downcast eyes, twisting the brim of his hat in his hands. "Maybe . . . maybe I should just come back another day," he said at last.

Gran nodded abruptly. "Mebbe so," she said.

9

I walked Jake back out to his car.

"Told you," I said.

He nodded. "Yeah, well . . . like I said, I can't blame her. To be honest, it's only a formality anyway. All the remaining lands were taken by eminent domain about a month ago."

My eyes bugged out.

"You mean, we don't own our house anymore?"

"Technically, no."

"Does Gran know that?"

"I suspect so. Legal notices were hand delivered to everyone affected."

I shook my head. "She never let on a word."

Jake smiled. "From what I just saw of your grandmother in there, I don't suppose she puts too much stock in legal notices."

I laughed. "You've got her pegged."

Jake laughed too. "Well," he said, "we'd like to tie things

up amicably if we can, get her signature on the bill of sale, make sure she gets what she's got coming to her. I'll try again another day."

"You know," I said slowly, remembering the house on the truck, "there might be one way of convincing her."

Jake turned to look at me. "Really?" he said. "Then I'd sure like to hear it."

"If there was a way to move the house," I said, "I think she might be more willing to go."

Jake stood back and surveyed the house thoughtfully. "That's one big house," he said. "They'd have to take it all apart, then put it back together again. And it looks like a lot of it would need to be repaired or re-placed. Could be done, but it'd cost a pretty penny."

I frowned. "That's what Mama said."

He nodded. "I'm afraid she's right."

"But the MDWSC has a lot of money," I said. "If you really want Gran to leave…"

"Celie," Jake said, "*everybody* in this valley has to leave. The MDWSC will give your grandmother a fair price for her house, based on its condition, just like we've done for everybody else. We can't do more than that. It wouldn't be right to do for one what we haven't done for others, would it?"

I sighed. "I s'pose not."

"Believe me," Jake added gently, "I don't like this part of my job any better than you do."

I nodded.

"I have to get going," Jake said. "I'll come back and see your grandmother again in a few days." He threw a leg over the door of his car, hopped in, and slid down behind the steering wheel.

"Okay," I said. "Don't forget about my ride."

"I won't." He smiled, then he looked up at me again. "Say, you wouldn't know where I could rent a room, would you? I was planning to stay at the Swift River Hotel, but they're going to start tearing it down this week."

My heart gave a little lurch. "They are?"

"Yes." He nodded. "I'm sorry. You didn't know?"

I shook my head. "No, I didn't."

"Must be kind of scary watching your town slowly disappear, huh?"

"Yeah." I nodded. "Sometimes I envy the people who have already left. They don't have to see it."

"Has your grandmother made any plans at all?" Jake asked.

I shrugged. "Not that I know of."

"How about you and your mom?"

"We go where Gran goes."

Jake nodded. "Well, good luck."

"Thanks."

Jake started his engine. It purred like a big kitten.

"Hey," I said suddenly. "We've got a room out over the carriage house that used to belong to our farmhand."

Jake looked interested for a moment, but then he laughed. "I've probably got about as much chance of renting that as I do of sprouting wings and flying."

I smiled. "I s'pose you're right about that."

He tipped his hat and started to back up.

"Stop in at the post office and ask Mr. Howell," I called after him. "He knows everything that's going on in Enfield."

Jake gave me a salute, then turned his MG toward town. I watched until the car was a little yellow speck in the distance.

Mama came walking up the hill and strolled across the lawn. She had a grocery sack in her arms.

"Who was that?" she asked.

"Did you see him, Mama?" I blurted. "Wasn't he just the bee's knees?"

Mama smiled. "Can't say as I got that close a look. What did he want?"

"He's with the MDWSC."

"Oh." She rolled her eyes. "Did Gran tar and feather him?"

I nodded. "Pretty much."

Mama shook her head. "Stubborn old woman. She can't fight city hall. None of us can. I don't know when she's going to realize that."

"Aren't *you* sad about leaving Enfield, Mama?" I asked.

Mama sighed. "Well, of course I am," she said, "but we've got to be practical, Celie. That water's comin' and nothing's going to stop it, least of all some ornery old woman."

I looked down at Enfield, nestled like a baby chick in the bosom of the hills. "I'm going to miss it here," I said softly. "I'm going to miss it bad."

"We all will, Celie," Mama said, "but it's time we got on with life." She slid an arm around my shoulders and guided me back toward the porch. "Besides, I've been thinking, maybe it won't be the worst thing, leaving here."

I looked at her skeptically and saw an unexpected spark in her eyes. She sat her grocery sack on the porch swing and pulled a letter from her pocket.

"Do you know what this is?" she asked.

I shook my head.

"It's a letter from my cousin Ruth in Chicago."

I looked at her blankly.

Mama sat down on the swing and pulled me down beside her. "When we were girls," she said excitedly, "we loved to make clothes for our dolls. We always talked of opening a dress shop together when we grew up, of creating our own designs and selling them. Well . . ." Mama hesitated. "Life had . . . other plans for me, but Ruth did it. She moved to Chicago and started out working in another woman's shop, then, in time, she opened her own."

I continued to stare at her blankly, wondering what all that had to do with us.

"I wrote to her, Celie," Mama said breathlessly, "and she answered. She says she'll give me a chance. I'll have to prove my worth, of course. Times are tough, even for Ruth. But I think I can do it, Celie. I know I'm a bit rusty, but I'm going to start practicing. . . ."

I tried to make sense of Mama's words as she rambled on.

"You mean . . . she's going to send you work to do here?" I asked.

"No," said Mama. "She wants us to come to Chicago."

"Chicago!" I nearly choked. "But Chicago is halfway across the country!"

"I know." Mama shivered a little. "It's kind of scary, but exciting, too, don't you think? Chicago is such a big town, bustling with department stores and picture shows, and big modern buildings. . . ."

"Picture shows?" I mumbled.

"Yes," said Mama. "You're always talking about how you wish we had a movie house in town. This is our chance, Celie, don't you see? You could even see that *Gone with the Wind* movie soon as it comes out, just like you've been wanting."

My buried rock was shooting up out of the ground like a volcano. "Well, that would be nice," I said, "but—what about our friends. What about *Chubby*? I'll never see him again."

"Of course you will," said Mama. "You'll keep in touch. You can write, maybe even phone once in a while."

Write? Phone? What kind of friendship is that?

"But, what about Gran?" I argued. "I don't think Gran would be happy in some big, modern town. I think she'll want to stay as close to the valley as she can."

Mama sighed, and the light went out of her eyes. "I know," she said heavily. She put her chin in her hand and rested her elbow on the arm of the swing. "I haven't figured that part out yet." She stared glumly across the valley.

I watched her, trying to read what was going on inside her head. "You really don't want to live around here anymore, do you?" I asked.

Mama looked at me apologetically. "No," she said. "I don't."

"But . . . why?" I asked. "This valley has always been our home. How can you want to leave it?"

Mama shook her head. "It's always been *your* home," she said. "You forget that I had a life before I came here. I grew up in a city, a small one, but a city nonetheless. And I loved it. Cities are so full of life, Celie. You can't even imagine."

I slumped back in the swing and crossed my arms.

"How can I make you understand?" Mama asked. "I *do* want to get away." She swept her hand across the far horizon. "I want to go *out there*, see new things, meet new people, make new friends. . . ."

There was a wistful tone to Mama's voice that I wasn't

sure I'd ever heard before. I looked into her eyes and suddenly saw her not as Mama, but as a woman. She was fairly young yet, in her midthirties, and still pretty, especially when she dressed up. She kept herself trim and fit, and whenever she went into town, she dressed as stylishly as we could afford. She always took pains with her hair, too, and wore lipstick, even when she was only working around the house. I wondered what it had been like for her all these years, widowed so young—left with a baby and an old woman in a town that was slowly dying. . . .

"Haven't you ever been happy living here, Mama?" I asked.

"Well, sure I have," she said. "I loved this valley when your daddy first brought me here. It was so peaceful and green, and we had such big plans. . . ." Mama's eyes went all faraway and misty. "Your daddy was going to get the farm up and running at full capacity again. We were going to have a bunch of babies. . . ." She pushed back a strand of her bobbed, golden hair, then sighed. "Lord, that seems a million years ago."

"What about after he died?" I asked quietly.

"After he died?" Mama paused and fixed her eyes on the distant hills again. "After he died it seemed like all the dreams died with him. And then the reservoir came along and the Depression hit, and this valley started dying too. To be honest, Celie . . ." She looked over at me. "Sometimes I got to feeling like I was dying right along with it."

I swallowed Mama's words a little at a time, seeing how they settled. "Why did you stay if you felt that way?" I asked.

"How could I take you away from Gran?" she asked me. "We were all she had left. Besides, where would I go? My mama and daddy still had eight younger ones at home. They didn't need any more mouths to feed."

"You could have gotten a job," I said.

Mama nodded slowly. "I could've," she said, "but to be honest, I was frightened. I didn't know if I could make it on my own with a little baby to care for."

I lowered my head. I had been so selfish, never thinking about Mama. Never realizing . . .

"And then, after a while," Mama continued quietly, "life fell into a routine, and I just kept going along and going along. . . ."

Her voice trailed off so sadly that I looked up at her with concern.

"Now don't get me wrong," she added, reading the worry in my eyes. "Gran's been real good to me . . . to us. And it's been a nice life, living here. But . . . maybe this reservoir is giving us the push we need to leave the valley and all its . . . ghosts, a chance to start over. Don't you think you might like that, Celie?"

I sat silent, pondering this new side of Mama. It was a jolt to realize that there was so much more to her than I'd ever known, that she had dreams and hopes of her own. Lord, maybe she'd even like to marry again someday. And who could blame her? She had a right to happiness. Part of me felt for Mama, wanted to be generous, to understand and support her. But the bigger part of me loved the quiet sameness, the comfortable rituals of my life, loved it being just us three— Gran and Mama and me.

"Celie?"

Mama was still watching me, awaiting my answer.

"I don't know," I said quietly. "I need time to think."

Mama squeezed my hand. "Okay," she said softly. "You take your time. I know this is all sudden and new to you. . . ."

"What's new to her?" Gran came walking round the corner from the backyard with her gardening hat on and a rake in her hand.

Mama straightened. "Oh, nothing," she said, giving me a wink. "What are you doing with that rake, Gran?"

"Now, what do you think I'm doin' with a rake?"

Mama smiled. "Okay. What are you raking?" she asked.

"The old leaves from last year," says Gran, "just like I do every spring. It's near time to put my pansies in."

Mama rolled her eyes. "Don't you think it's time to stop all this foolishness, Gran?" she said. "We really have to start making plans. . . ."

Gran stiffened and shot Mama a look fit to kill. Mama quit talking midsentence and threw her hands up. "All right. Suit yourself then," she said. "I'll just shut my mouth and we'll all go right on pretending." She picked up her grocery sack and stomped into the house.

Gran put her head down and attacked the flower beds with a vengeance.

"I'll help you, Gran," I said.

"Nope." Gran sniffed. "Don't need no help. I'm just a foolish old woman wastin' my time and I don't need no help."

I smiled and went to get another rake.

10

Mama stuck her head in at my bedroom door. "Hustle up, now," she said. "Gran's still in a snit over that water commission fella yesterday, and it won't help things around here none if we're late for church on top of it."

She disappeared again, and I looked at Ginger curled up cozily in the middle of my quilt. "You're lucky you're a cat," I said. "Nobody ever rushes you. Nobody makes you go to church or school. I think in my next life I want to be a cat."

As if to taunt me further, Ginger stretched luxuriously, her little pink tongue curling out in a big yawn, then she rolled over and went back to sleep.

I slipped my dress over my head, buckled my Sunday shoes, and bolted down the stairs, leaping over the last three and landing with a thump at the bottom.

"My lands, Cecelia," said Gran, "you sound like a herd of wild elephants, and where are your gloves?" Gran wouldn't think of going to town without gloves and a hat.

"I don't want to wear 'em," I said. "Gloves aren't modern, Gran."

"Modern?" Gran glared at me as if I'd grown another head. "I'll give you *modern*, young lady. You march right back upstairs and get those gloves on this minute. No granddaughter of mine is going to set foot in church without her gloves."

I turned with a huff and stomped back up the stairs.

"I swear these young people today are all goin' to hell in a handbasket," I heard Gran grumbling to herself.

A horn sounded outside.

"I declare," Gran called out, "what is *that* bellowin' now?"

Mama bustled out of her room with her hat in her hand. "Oh, I nearly forgot," she shouted down the stairs. "It's Tom Kessler, come by to give us a ride to church."

"Keen!" I cried.

Gran would never let us have a car, so it was always a treat for me to ride in one, even Tom Kessler's old wreck of a Model T. I ran into my room, snatched up my gloves, and dashed back downstairs. Mama and Gran were in the midst of a "discussion."

"It's a fine day for walkin'," Gran snapped. "Since when do we need a ride?"

"Since Tom offered when I saw him in town yesterday," said Mama. "I thought it was very kind of him, so I accepted."

Gran sniffed. "These young people and their automobiles," she said. "Think they got to drive everywhere. Nobody walks anymore. Mind you, sooner or later babies'll be born with no legs a'tal."

Mama pinned her hat on her head and primped her hair in the front hall mirror. "I guess that's a chance we'll have to take, Gran," she said, giving me a sidelong wink.

The horn sounded again.

"Will you just listen to that man?" Gran clucked her tongue. "Sitting out there blowing his horn like a bull elephant? Does he expect we're going to parade out there like pigs called to slop? If he wants to escort us to church, he will come callin' like a proper gentleman. And we will sit right here until he does."

Frankly, Gran didn't have much use for Tom Kessler. He was one of the new folks that had come to town to work on the dam. He was renting a house up the street, and I think he was a little sweet on Ma. I didn't think Ma was much interested in him, though. He was nice enough, but plain as puddin' and dull as a butter knife.

"Gran," Mama explained, "Tom's engine is acting up some. He's afraid it'll stall if he gets out of the car, and he has trouble starting it up again when it's warm."

"Well, I'd far sooner walk to church than be called out of my house like a pig to slop," Gran insisted. "If you've got no more pride than that, you kin just go on ahead without me."

Mama sighed and marched out of the house, and Gran sat down on the parlor sofa and folded her arms. Before long Tom came in, offered her his arm, and escorted her out to the car. That's Gran for you when she got her mind made up about something.

Well, of course the car stalled, and it took quite a few cranks for Tom to get it going again, and being it was unseasonably warm, he looked quite sweaty and rumpled by the time he climbed back into the front seat. He didn't appear one bit pleased, but at least we were finally off. We rattled and bumped all the way to church, which was actually held in the grange hall, since the real church had burned down two years previous.

"Lucky thing I don't have false teeth," Gran grumbled under her breath. "This car'd knock 'em right out of my head."

I hung out the window and waved to everybody we passed along the way, but Gran sat ramrod straight with her hands folded in her lap. Gran never did handle progress real well.

When we got to the center of town my mood abruptly changed. They had taken a whole row of shops down just since Friday. The shops had been empty for some time, of course, but it was still a shock to see them gone, nothing left but a pile of rubble. The meat market was gone, and Mrs. Roger's Dry Goods, and Campbell's Bakery. . . . A lump rose in my throat. How many times had Chubby and I hurried to Campbell's after school to stare longingly at the baked goods in the hope that Herb Campbell would offer us something from the day-old shelf? How many times had Herb chased us out and told us we were driving away the paying customers? I smiled sadly. I was going to miss Mr. Campbell.

Up ahead was the Swift River Hotel, already missing a chunk of its roof. The demolition teams had started dismantling it. Gran never took her eyes from the building as we drove by. She said nothing, but I could see the muscles of her jaw working, and I knew she was fighting back tears. The hotel had been so much a part of the town all these years, the scene of so many weddings and balls and parties. It was hard to believe that within a few days it, too, would be reduced to a pile of rubble.

Chubby was waiting for me outside of church. I almost didn't recognize him at first. It seemed like he'd shot up another couple of inches overnight. Ma sure was right. He wasn't a bit chubby anymore. He'd grown at least a foot since the seventh grade, and all his baby fat had kind of moved around and rearranged itself into muscle. I wished puberty had been as kind to me. I'd grown tall all right. I was already five foot eight—too tall for a girl, a lot of folks said, but I didn't think so. I liked being tall, but unfortunately I was also skinny as a stick and had no bosoms at all to speak of. Mama and Gran were always shoving food at me, and I ate it, too, but it seemed totally disinclined to do anything but make me taller.

"Why so glum?" asked Chubby when he saw me.

"Did you see Campbell's?" I asked.

He nodded. "Yeah. Stinks, huh?"

I nodded too.

We filed into church behind Mama and Gran. There were only a handful of people in the seats. Every week there were fewer and fewer.

Mama and Tom and Gran took seats beside Aunt Stella. Aunt Stella wasn't really my aunt. She wasn't a relative at all, but she'd been Gran's best friend for fifty years, and I'd called her Aunt Stella all my life.

Chubby and I filed into an empty row behind them. Aunt Stella turned around and blew me a kiss. I blew one back.

"Oh brother," groaned Chubby, leaning in close to my ear. "I forgot to bring my earplugs, and look who's playing today."

I turned and saw Belinda Wilder sashaying up the aisle like Mae West, a roll of sheet music tucked under her arm.

"Nerts," I said. "Not again."

Miss Hanover, who had played the organ for forty-seven years, never missing a Sunday, had moved away in February. Reverend Marsh had asked if anyone else could play, and none other than Belinda Wilder had raised her hand. She'd hit so many sour notes that first Sunday it was all we could do not to cover our ears, but none of the parishioners had the heart to complain, so she'd been playing most every Sunday since.

She paused at the end of our aisle. "Good morning, Chubby," she said, batting her eyelashes. "Is there anything special you'd like me to play this morning?"

"Yeah. How about if you play 'Far, Far Away'?" said Chubby.

"Or why don't you play 'By the Window' and I'll help you out," I put in. Chubby and I dissolved into giggles.

Belinda put her nose in the air. "You are *such* juveniles," she huffed. Then she wiggled on up the aisle.

In truth it gave me great pleasure to see the way the other parishioners cringed when she took her seat on the bench. She arranged her music and started banging on the keys, playing something . . . none of us knew what . . . until Reverend Marsh walked in, loudly singing "Rock of Ages." The rest of us opened our songbooks and joined in, trying our best to drown out the organ.

Reverend Marsh preached to us a sermon from Psalm 91:

He who dwells in the shelter of the Most High, who abides in the shadow of the Almighty will say to the Lord, "My refuge and my fortress: my God, in whom I trust." For he will deliver you from the snare of the fowler and from the deadly pestilence; he will cover you with his pinions, and under his wings

*you will find refuge. . . . Because you have made the Most
High your habitation, no evil shall befall you, no scourge shall
come near your tent.*

Gran listened raptly and seemed to draw strength from
the service. I think Reverend Marsh meant for his words to
give us consolation about having to leave our homes, but I
had a feeling it was the "no scourge shall come near your
tent" part that Gran took to heart. And I had a further feeling that in her mind she was spelling *scourge M-D-W-S-C.*

Mama and Tom, and Gran and Aunt Stella stood outside
after the service, talking with Chubby's parents and some of
the other neighbors, and Chubby and I stood politely by and
listened, but it was the same old talk: who was moving where
and when. Depressing. At last Chubby's mother called to
him that it was time to go home for dinner.

"Coming," said Chubby, then he led me a little bit away
from the crowd. "It's so nice and warm. Whaddya say we go
fishin' up to Greenwich Lake after dinner?" he asked.

"Sure," I whispered. We had to keep such plans quiet
because we were forbidden to poke around the demolition
sites, and they'd been doing a lot of work up toward the lake
lately.

"I'll come by around twelve-thirty," Chubby said.

"I'll be waiting."

I was anxious to get home and get dinner over with after
that, but it took me another ten minutes to drag Gran and
Mama away from Aunt Stella, and then the drive home
seemed to take forever. The roads were clogged with Sunday
sightseers. Tom kept layin' on his *ow-oo-gah* horn, but it

seemed like nobody was in a hurry but us. It probably would have been faster to walk.

Gran stared out her window at the hordes of people come to ogle the demolition. "Vultures," she whispered under her breath.

We were halfway up Great Quabbin Hill, almost to our house, when Gran suddenly yelled, "Stop!"

Tom slammed on his brakes, and I slid off of my seat and landed in a heap on the floor. "What's wrong?" Tom asked impatiently.

"Let me out!" cried Gran. She was banging the door with her prayer book and fighting with the handle. Tom hopped out and ran around to open the door and help her down. Without another word, Gran took off at a trot across our next-door neighbors', the Hanovers', front lawn.

"You!" she yelled. "You there! What d'ya think you're doin'?"

Suddenly we saw what it was that had got her goat. The Hanover house had been empty for some time. The whole family had moved to Athol just before Christmas, and they'd been going back and forth ever since, moving their stuff little by little to the new place. They had the house pretty well cleaned out, but the barn was still full. Some strangers had managed to get the barn door open and were poking through the things the Hanovers had left behind. They had their arms full of tools.

Tom started across the yard after Gran, and Mama and I followed.

"What're you doin' there?" Gran shouted at the strangers again.

The men barely glanced at her. "What business is it of yours?" one of them called back.

Gran marched right into their midst and put her hands on her hips.

"I'll tell you what business it is of mine," she said. "This is my neighbor's prope'ty and I'm lookin' out for it."

"Ain't nobody livin' here no more," one man said.

Gran was close to boiling over. "You put everthin' down and git out of here right now," she shouted, "or so help me I'll whale the tarnation oughta the lot of you!"

The men didn't move, and the next thing we knew, Gran started swinging at them with her purse.

"Git outa here," she cried. "Right now!"

"Hey! Hey!" the men shouted, dropping the tools and covering their heads with their arms. "Cut that out, you crazy old bat."

"I'll crazy-old-bat *you!*" cried Gran. She threw the purse at one of them, then picked up a scythe and started swinging it at their feet.

"Hey, *hey!*" they shouted, jumping around. "All right! *All right!* We're going!" They fled from the barn, cursing and grumbling.

"Geez," one said as he hightailed it past us. "That old dame belongs in a nuthouse!"

Tom, who was pretty big, and could be mighty mean-looking when he wanted to be, scowled his meanest scowl. "She's a lady, not a dame," he said. "And if you don't want no trouble, you better do as she says."

"Bunch of hillbillies, the lot of ya," another man shouted as they climbed back into their truck.

"And don't let me see yer faces around here again," Gran

shouted, still brandishing her scythe, "or I'll have the law down on you!"

Mama shook her head at Gran in amused admiration, then she turned to Tom. "Thank you kindly for your help, and for the ride, Tom," she said. "We can walk home from here."

Tom hesitated a moment, glancing at me awkwardly.

"Was there something you wanted to say, Tom?" Mama asked.

Tom glanced at me again, then he pulled his hat off and clutched it to his chest. He looked at Mama and his face turned red as a rooster comb.

"Well, Miss Helen," he said hesitantly, "it was just that . . . I was wonderin' if maybe you had plans to go to the Fireman's Ball come Wednesday."

Mama smiled. "Why I wouldn't miss it," she said.

Tom looked even more flustered. "What I meant was, well, if you don't already have plans . . . I thought maybe . . . well. . . ."

Mama grinned and laid her hand gently on Tom's arm. "I'd be pleased to go with you, Tom," she said.

Tom's face lit up brighter than sunshine on snow.

"Well, good then," he said, breaking into a grin. "I'll be lookin' forward to it then."

"As will I," said Mama.

Tom replaced his hat and bid us good day, then he headed back toward his car with a bit of a skip in his step.

Mama smothered a giggle. "He's such a sweet man," she said, shaking her head.

I looked from Mama to Tom and back, wonderingly. Could it be that Mama *was* interested in Tom? I turned to see what Gran was making of this little scene, but she was busy, carefully, almost lovingly, replacing the tools on their hooks. I went to give her a hand.

"Tools say a lot about a man," Gran said when I came up. "See how these are cared for, Celie—cleaned and oiled, the blades honed and sharp? Not a speck of rust or dirt anywhere? Hiram Hanover is a good man. A good neighbor. Back when your granddaddy first died, Hiram took on my chores in addition to his own. Never asked if I needed help. Just did what he knew needed doin'. Your daddy helped, too, of course, but he was just a boy then 'bout your age, and he had his schoolin' to tend to. I don't know how we'd have managed without Hiram. He pitched in for the better part of a year, till I got your granddaddy's affairs in order and found me a farmhand."

Gran ran her small, wrinkled hand along the smooth, worn shaft of Hiram Hanover's scythe. "Where am I s'posed to find me a neighbor like that again?" she asked quietly.

11

Chubby came for me just as we were finishing up dinner.

"Can I be excused, Mama?" I asked.

"Go along," said Mama, "but change out of your Sunday dress first."

"Can I wear my overalls?" I asked.

Gran's eyes popped. "Overalls?" she said. "Why? Are you plannin' on shovelin' manure?"

Chubby laughed.

"No," I said. "They're just more comfortable is all."

Gran snorted. "What has comfort to do with anything?" she asked. "Pants b'long on boys and dresses on girls, and that's the way of it."

"Lots of girls wear pants these days, Gran," I said. "It's modern."

Gran brushed my words away like they were a swarm of gnats. "Modern my foot," she mumbled.

I looked beseechingly at Mama, but she just shrugged. Mama picked her battles with Gran, and obviously she wasn't picking this one.

"Marlene Dietrich wears pants," I said, "and she's a glamorous movie star."

"She's a character," said Gran. "Anybody'll tell you that."

"Well, I want to be a character too," I said.

Gran cracked a smile. "You're well on yer way," she said.

"So I can wear 'em?" I asked hopefully.

"You can wear 'em when pigs fly," said Gran.

Chubby laughed again. "C'mon, Celie," he said. "Time's wastin'. Besides, your Gran's right." He puffed out his chest. "Everybody knows it's men should wear the pants."

I shot him a warning glance. "I'd stay out of this if I were you, Chubby Miller," I snapped.

Chubby threw his hands up in surrender. "Just trying to be helpful," he said. "But I know when I'm not wanted. I'll be waiting outside."

I huffed upstairs to change, then stomped through the kitchen on my way out. Gran smiled approvingly when she saw my skirt. "You mind what I told you about boys and bulls, now," she warned. "Can't help themselves, y'know. It's in their genes."

I smiled. "Yes, Gran. I'll remember."

Mama took note of the sweater I was carrying under my arm. "Mite warm for a sweater," she said with a merry glint in her eye.

"Afternoons still get chilly this time of year," I replied, then I scooted out the door before Gran got suspicious.

"Supper's at six," Mama called after me.

Gran didn't hold with girls riding bicycles, so we had to

walk Chubby's bike until we were out of sight. Then I ducked behind a tree, changed into my overalls, and hopped up on his handlebars. I started to whistle "Sweet Georgia Brown" as Chubby rode me through town. He clucked his tongue disapprovingly.

"Whistling girls and crowing hens never come to any good end," he teased.

I laughed. "Okay, *Gran*," I said.

"Doesn't she about drive you screwy with all her old-fashioned rules?" Chubby asked.

I shrugged. "Sometimes. Mostly I manage to keep her happy and do what I want too."

"Ever get caught?" Chubby asked.

"Just that once," I said, "when she found me trying out that cigarette behind the barn."

"Oh yeah," Chubby chuckled. "I remember that."

"Not as well as I do," I said. "She made me eat it! Killed my taste for cigarettes, I'll tell you that."

Chubby laughed out loud. "Jeepers creepers," he said. "She's one feisty old lady, huh?"

"Yeah." I smiled. "I like her like that, though. I'm going to be one feisty old lady when I get her age too."

Chubby nodded. "Got no doubt about that," he said.

It was uncommonly warm and the breeze felt good in my face. We stopped at Chubby's father's filling station, and Chubby lifted the lid of the big red Coca-Cola cooler and fished us two sodas out of the icy water. We gulped them thirstily, then he ran around back to get his fishing pole. I waited out front with the bike.

Strangers strolled up and down the streets of town, snapping pictures of the torn-down buildings and kicking through the rubble, looking for souvenirs. A little girl looked up at me like I was some sort of oddity.

"Do you live here?" she asked, wide-eyed.

"Yes," I said.

"Did they tear your house down yet?" she asked.

I swallowed hard.

"Nellie," said the little girl's mother, "don't be rude." She hustled the child away.

"Hey there," someone called. "Isn't that Miss Celie Wheeler?"

I turned to see two adorable Clark Gable dimples smiling at me.

"Hello! Mr. . . . uh Jake. How are you?"

"Just fine," said Jake. He nodded at the bike. "Nice day for a ride. Where you headed?"

"Um . . . nowhere in particular."

Jake was in shirtsleeves and looked charmingly disheveled.

"Did you find a place to stay?" I asked.

He ran a hand through his hair, then pulled at his chin, which sported a stubbly shadow of beard. "I look a sight, I suppose." He chuckled self-consciously. "Spent the night in my car."

"Oh," I winced. "That's terrible."

"Well, it's not *that* bad," he said. "I've slept in worse places. Kinda tough on the back, though. I hope I find something by tonight."

"Didn't Mr. Howell have any ideas?" I asked.

Jake shook his head. "The only places left are already full up with the construction and demolition teams."

"Hey, Celie. You ready?" Chubby motioned to me from over by the gas pump.

Jake glanced at him. "Oh," he said. "I'm sorry. I didn't realize you were with someone."

"It's okay," I said with a shrug. "He's just a friend."

"Well, I don't want to interfere with your plans," said Jake. "You kids run along. I'm sure I'll find something." He started to walk away.

The word *kids* grated on me. I didn't want Jake thinking of me as a kid. "Wait," I said.

He turned around.

"Look," I told him, "we've got that whole room just sitting out there in the carriage house. It's not right for you to have to sleep in your car. I'll talk to my grandmother. You come by tonight after supper."

Jake arched one eyebrow skeptically. "I don't want to make any more trouble for you," he said.

"Don't worry about me," I told him, squaring my shoulders. "I can take care of myself. Besides, Gran's bark is worse than her bite."

Jake shrugged. "Okay," he said. "I'll stop by around seven then. Tell her I'm more than happy to pay anything she thinks fair."

"I'll tell her. Bye, Jake."

"Bye, Celie." He gave me one of his charming winks, then turned and walked away. I stared after him, dreamy eyed.

"Hey." Chubby had come up beside me. "Who was that?"

"Works for the MDWSC," I said. "Isn't he swell?"

"Swell? Looks like a drugstore cowboy to me."

"He is not," I said. "He's nice as pie."

Chubby slipped his pole into the holster he'd rigged for it on the back of his bike and we started walking, weaving in and out among the sightseers.

"What's he doin' hangin' around you then, besides tryin' to make a little time?"

"That's pure banana oil, Chubby Miller," I said, secretly enjoying Chubby's concern. "He came by yesterday to talk to Gran, and I just bumped into him again on the street, that's all."

"That so?" said Chubby.

"Yes, that's so," I insisted, "so you can just get off your high horse and mind your own business."

Chubby raised his eyebrows. "What are you getting all flustered about?" he asked. "You stuck on him or something?"

"What? Of course not!"

Chubby grinned. "Then why are you turning red?"

"I am doing nothing of the kind."

"Are too. He's a little old for you, don't you think?"

I snorted and stomped off. "Chubby Miller, you are the most annoying person on the face of this earth!" I shouted back over my shoulder.

Chubby hopped on his bike and caught up with me in two seconds.

"What's his name anyway?" he asked.

"None of your business," I snapped, refusing to look at him.

"C'mon, tell me."

"Why? So you can tease me some more?"

"I'm just curious," he said. "I'm sorry. I won't tease you anymore."

"You're lying."

"No, I'm not. Cross my heart and hope to die."

I huffed. "Oh, all right. It's Jake if you must know."

"Jeepers," said Chubby. "First name basis, huh? Sounds like you two are getting kind of chummy." He tilted his head back and started singing at the top of his lungs, "Jake and Celie sitting in a tree, *k-i-s-s-i-n-g*."

My jaw dropped and I spun around, praying that Jake was out of earshot. Thankfully, he was nowhere in sight.

"Jake and Celie . . . Chubby repeated, even louder than before.

I put my hands over my ears and started to run.

"Chubby Miller, I *hate* you!" I screamed.

12

"Aw c'mon, Celie," Chubby begged. "Give it up, will ya?"

"Go cook a radish," I snapped as I strutted along, still refusing to look his way.

"Don't be such a poor sport," he said. "You tease me all the time and I don't get my knickers in a twist. . . ."

He went on whining and cajoling, but I had stopped listening. We were traveling the old railroad bed that snaked through the gap between Little Quabbin Hill and Prescott Ridge. As the scenery unfolded before me, my stomach balled up in a knot. Even though I should have known what to expect, I was unprepared for what I saw. Prescott Ridge, usually snowy with apple blossoms this time of year, had been shaved. Nothing remained of its beautiful orchards but a stubble of stumps. The green pastures of Little Quabbin Hill had been plowed under. Gone were the cows that usually grazed there, meandering up and down the hillside with their wobbly calves following behind. Alongside the tracks, where the east branch of the Swift River used to run, deep and rushing this time of year, only a dry, dusty gulch remained. The ancient trees that used to line its banks were now just ugly stumps. And these had been my favorites—the willows. In the spring, when they turned yellow, they had always reminded me of maidens washing their long, golden hair in the water.

Instead of the sweet smell of apple blossoms drifting on the breeze, there was nothing but dust and dirt. It swept in clouds across the barren landscape, making my eyes water and coating my teeth with grit.

A little farther on we passed Smith's Village, and it was more of the same—the countryside butchered, like a newsreel scene from the Great War. Gone were the mills and the post office. Gone were the meadows and the cozy farmhouses. Gone were the men working in the fields and the women hanging wash in their backyards. Gone were the kids racing down the rutted lanes, or hanging by their knees in the apple trees. All that remained were cellar holes and empty roadbeds, stacks of logs and piles of brush. Soon Enfield would look like this. My throat felt raw and ragged, and tears began to slip down my cheeks. I sniffed hard to hold them back.

"Celie?" Chubby's voice was edged with concern. "Celie, are you crying? Geez, I didn't think you'd get this upset. . . ."

"It's not you!" I shouted, stopping in my tracks and turning at last to look at him. "It's—" I swept my arm in an arc across the horizon. "It's *this*."

Chubby stopped, too, and stared. "I know," he said quietly. "I know."

I sniffed and wiped my eyes.

"C'mon," said Chubby, "hop on. It's not as bad up around the lake yet."

I gave in and climbed back onto his handlebars. The bike jounced and wiggled as he pedaled along the hard-packed clay of the bumpy old track bed. We didn't speak until Greenwich Lake came into sight, still rimmed in green, standing like an oasis in the middle of the devastation.

"I wonder why they haven't cleared out around the lake yet?" I asked.

"Don't know," said Chubby. "Maybe some of the rich folks are holding up the works."

I nodded. "S'pose so."

A lot of wealthy people from Boston and New York had summerhouses on Greenwich Lake. They weren't allowed to live in them anymore, but I guessed maybe people were still moving stuff out, or even moving the houses themselves.

When we reached the lake we saw that a lot of the houses were gone already, but a few remained. It was eerily quiet. Usually this time of year the lake bustled with activity—folks opening up their camps, greeting old friends, repairing the winter's damage. . . . Today there wasn't a soul in sight—just a few birds singing in the trees, and a beaver trying to dam up Gibbs Brook where it flowed into the lake.

"I wonder what'll become of the animals," I said.

"You don't have to worry about them," Chubby assured me. "The water will rise slow enough that they'll keep moving higher. And the watershed is going to be like a big game preserve. They'll be just fine."

"Well, that's good at least," I mumbled.

"Hey, kiddo." Chubby yanked playfully on one of my braids. "Don't be such a sob sister, huh? It's a beautiful day. Let's enjoy it."

I sighed and nodded.

I hopped off the bike, and Chubby put his kickstand down and took his pole out.

"C'mon," he said. "Nothing like fishin' to take your mind off things."

I had never really shared Chubby's enthusiasm for the sport of fishing, but I found it relaxing to be with him when he did it. We made our way along the bank to his favorite spot, a large, flat boulder that some ancient glacier had rolled down Mount Pomeroy and left resting on the shore. It was a popular perch for sunbathers and fisherman alike. Today it was deserted, though, and Chubby and I had it all to ourselves. I sat down on the rock while Chubby checked over his gear. He handed me his tackle box.

"Pick me out a fly," he said while he worked at a knot in his line. I poked through his tackle box, looking over the dozens of assorted flies that Chubby and I had tied on long winter afternoons, all the while dreaming of a spring day like this. I pulled out a mayfly nymph.

"Here," I said. "I tied this one. It'll bring you luck."

Chubby took the fly and secured it to his line, then he stood and made a few practice casts. I watched as the line snaked gracefully through the air. Then he cast in earnest and the line drifted, light as a silk thread, down, down toward the water until, just as the fly alighted, Chubby jerked it up again. Over and over he put the fly through this ballet, tempting the fish, drawing them up to the surface. I admired the way Chubby moved, like a maestro conducting a symphony. He was a master at this.

I watched a while longer, then I lay back on the rock and stared up at the sky. Puffy white clouds drifted by, changing and rearranging themselves into different shapes as they moved. I thought about Chubby and me and wondered what moving would do to us. Would it reshape us like the clouds, make us different people?

"Chubby?" I said suddenly.

"Yeah?"

"We'll always be friends, right? No matter what happens?"

Chubby looked over at me. "Of course," he said.

I sat up and drew my knees in tight, linking my arms around them. "But what if we move far away from each other?" I said. "It won't be the same."

Chubby snaked his line over his head and cast it out again. "Don't be silly," he said. "We're not going to move far away from each other. My daddy's got his eye on a filling station over in Warton. A lot of Enfield folks are moving there. I'm sure that's where you'll end up too."

I sighed. "I don't know," I told him. "Mama's taken a notion to move to Chicago."

"Chicago!" Chubby lowered his pole and turned to look at me. "What's in *Chicago?*"

"One of her cousins. She owns a dress shop. She's offered Mama a job."

Chubby's brow wrinkled with concern. "Do you think she'd leave your grandmother?" he asked.

"No." I shook my head. "I don't think she'd ever do that."

"Well then," said Chubby, brightening, "you know your grandmother isn't going to step one foot farther away from this town than is absolutely necessary, and if it comes down to a test of wills between your ma and your grandmother, my money's on your grandmother."

I smiled, feeling a little better, but I wasn't as sure as Chubby.

"I don't know," I said. "Mama really wants to start all over. She wants to live in a big city."

"What do you want?" Chubby asked.

"I want to stay here, of course," I said.

"Then you'll stay," Chubby said matter-of-factly. "Your ma won't make you move if she knows you and your grandmother both want to stay. I'll bet if she found a nice modern little house in Warton she'd be happy."

His confidence reassured me. I stretched back out in the sun again and closed my eyes, dreaming of a pretty piece of land on a hill in Warton. I pictured a cozy house, one of those kinds they call a Cape Cod, overlooking Sandy Pond, in walking distance of town and Chubby's daddy's filling station. In the dream, lots of my old friends lived nearby, too, and we all went to school together, and in the winter we skated on Sandy Pond, and in the summer we had picnics and hayrides. It was almost . . . almost as good as staying right in Enfield.

Soon the dream was so real that I had myself believing it. Mama *would* be happy there, I convinced myself, once she realized how nice it would be. There was a department store in Warton, and a movie house of sorts. It didn't get many big-name movies, but it was a movie house just the same. And there were sure to be plenty of new people to meet. . . .

I didn't know how long I'd been daydreaming, but my cheeks were beginning to pinch from the sun, and the heat pressing down on my overalls was making me perspire.

I sat up again. "It's downright *hot*," I said, mopping my forehead with my hand.

"Yeah," Chubby agreed. "It's gotta be in the eighties, I'll bet. Strange weather for April."

I looked at the cool, inviting water all around me. "I'm almost tempted to jump in," I said.

"Mmmm," Chubby mumbled absent-mindedly.

I giggled. "Remember when we were little, how we used to sneak off and go skinny-dipping?"

That caught Chubby's attention. "Yeah," he said, smiling at me with a mischievous glint in his eye. "Want to try it again? Nobody's around."

I laughed. "In your dreams, Chubby Miller."

Chubby shrugged. "What?" he said. "It's not like you got much to hide."

"Oh, and you do?"

"Wouldn't you like to know?" said Chubby with a wink.

I blushed in spite of myself, and Chubby laughed.

"Nerts!" he said suddenly. His lure had snagged up in a tree on the backswing of his cast. He yanked and yanked until finally, the line snapped.

"Some luck you brought me," he grumbled. He came over and bent close, poking through the tackle box for another lure. He smelled of Octagon soap and Burma-Shave. I thought about the things Gran had said about boys, and my heart quickened. As if he sensed something, Chubby suddenly looked up into my eyes.

"What's wrong?" he asked.

"Nothing," I said, but I could feel myself blushing again.

He kept looking at me strangely, and my breath seemed to catch in my throat.

"You're not fixing to kiss me, Chubby Miller, are you?" I blurted.

Chubby looked startled. "What?" he asked, turning red.

"Gran says teenage boys are like bulls in spring," I rushed on. "She says they can't help themselves. . . ."

Chubby blinked once or twice, then broke into a wide grin. "That so?" he said. "Well, maybe she's right." He started leaning closer.

I knew he was just trying to be funny, but my heart started thumping just the same. I'd never kissed a boy, but I'd dreamed about it a lot. I'd dreamed about a moment just like this. I stared at Chubby's mouth. It felt like a magnet, pulling my lips toward his, closer, closer. . . .

Then suddenly an alarm went off in my head. This was Chubby! This was my best friend. Best friends didn't kiss! He was teasing me, that was all. He'd never let me live it down if I actually kissed him.

"Cut it out!" I shouted, giving him a shove.

He staggered backward and nearly fell off the rock.

We looked at each other awkwardly, each trying to read the other, neither knowing quite what to say. Then he forced out a laugh. His ears were bright red.

"Like bulls," he said. "That's a good one."

I laughed, too, to cover my embarrassment. "I know," I said. "I told her there was nothing to worry about. I told her it wasn't like you were a *real* boy or anything."

Chubby's face fell. He stared at me in stunned silence for a long moment, then he frowned. "I *am* a real boy, Celie," he said quietly, then he picked up his rod, walked over to the farthest side of the rock, and sat down with his back to me.

13

On the way home it was Chubby's turn not to talk, and after a time I gave up trying to apologize. I knew Chubby well enough to know that he couldn't hold a grudge. By tomorrow all would be forgiven and we'd be back to normal. He dropped me in front of the Hanovers' house and wheeled away without saying good-bye. I changed out of my overalls, cut through the yards, and headed for our old dairy barn to ditch them before going up to the house. I pushed the door open and then my breath caught in my throat. Standing right in front of me was Gran.

"Gran!" I gasped. "What are you doing here?"

"Might ask you the same," said Gran. She looked down at the overalls in my hand.

"Um . . . I was . . . um . . ."

"Gonna shovel manure?" asked Gran.

My face turned red and I giggled. "You caught me," I said.

"I was going to ditch these here until I could sneak them back into my room."

"Should'a jest used the sweater again," said Gran.

My mouth dropped. "You knew?"

"Course I knew," said Gran. "Y'think I was born yesterday?"

"Then how come you let me go?" I asked.

Gran smiled coyly. "Because you remind me of m'self when I was your age," she said. "I wasn't always an old fuddy-duddy, y'know."

I grinned.

"But that don't mean you should go takin' advantage," Gran added, shaking her finger at me.

I laughed. "I won't, Gran," I promised.

The barn was warm and still but full of the ghosts of livelier days. The floors and walls exhaled sweet-and-sour memories of hay and milk, manure and sweat, oil and leather, birth and death. I threw my overalls and sweater over an old wooden peg, then climbed up the gate of one of the stalls and sat perched on top.

Gran clucked her tongue. "Mind, you have a skirt on now," she said, "not overalls. Good thing there's no menfolks around. I can see ever'thing you own."

I giggled. "Gran, you worry about the screwiest stuff," I said. "What're you doing out here anyway?"

"Just looking for a bucket," said Gran. "Mine sprung a leak. Thought there might be some old milking pails out here somewhere."

She went over and lifted the lid of one of the grain bins along the wall. She started rummaging through, pulling out old pieces of harness, ropes, and tools.

"Ah, here's one," she said. She lifted out a tin pail and sat it on the ground.

I stared at it and suddenly a memory floated up from somewhere deep inside me. It was my daddy, I think. I couldn't see his face, but I could see his hands pumping like pistons as milk *zing, zing, zinged* into the metal pail—white hands, not brown, so they had to be Daddy's and not Cal's. And I remembered the taste of milk—creamy, rich, and warm.

"Gran," I said, "did Daddy used to bring me here with him when he was milking?"

"'Course he did. Your daddy took you everywhere," said Gran. "You loved the barn—used to toddle around, chasing kittens while he milked." Gran chuckled. "One day you watched him squirt a stream of milk right into the mouth of one of the cats," she went on. "Next thing he knew, you wanted some too. You toddled over with your mouth open like a little bird's, and he gave you a squirt. Well, that was the end of it. Every time he milked thereafter, you had to have your share. In the summertime, when you were dressed in just your little diaper, he'd miss on purpose sometimes and squirt you right in the belly. And you'd laugh. My, how you'd laugh." Gran's eyes sparkled with the memory.

"I remember, Gran," I said softly. "Not clear memories, but when I'm in here I remember the *feel* of Daddy."

Gran nodded, then she looked around. "Oh, he's here," she said quietly, "and your granddaddy too. This barn is soaked with the sweat of their backs, shaped by the skill of their hands. It bore witness to their dreams and disappointments, and when times got the hardest, it was these rafters heard their desperate prayers."

Gran sniffed and picked up a piece of harness. She

caressed the leather, still supple after all these years, still dark with neat's-foot oil. "That's what those folks in Boston don't understand," she said, her voice husky with emotion. "These aren't just buildin's they're tearin' down. They're people's lives."

I stared at the sparkling dust motes drifting in the shaft of late-day sun that slanted down from the high barn windows. It still didn't seem real, didn't seem possible that before long this barn would be gone, and with it, my deep, buried memories of Daddy.

"Can I have that milking pail when you're done with it, Gran?" I asked.

"What for?" asked Gran.

"I just want to keep it," I said, "forever."

Gran nodded slowly. "Sure enough, dear," she said. "That'd please your daddy." Then she sighed. "Come give me a hand putting this stuff back in the bin. It must be gettin' on toward suppertime."

Mama had supper waiting for us—leftover ham from dinner, with potato salad and baking powder biscuits. I ate hungrily while Gran and Mama chattered on about Lucille Thatcher's wedding. Lucille and her beau, Harry Webber, were getting married in June, and since it would likely be the last wedding ever held in Enfield, the whole town was invited. They were going to hold the wedding on the Webber's front lawn, since the church had burned down and the grange just wasn't all that pretty a place for a wedding.

"It's a shame there aren't enough of the ladies left to hold a quilting bee," Gran fretted as we washed up the dishes. "Just don't seem right to send a young bride off without a quilt."

"Things are changing, Gran," Mama said.

"Not for the better, I'll tell you that," Gran grumbled.

Mama's mood abruptly darkened. "How would you know," she huffed at Gran, "when you won't give progress half a chance?"

Gran glared at her, and neither said another word until the grandfather clock in the front hall clock started striking seven. Suddenly I remembered my promise to Jake.

"Oh my gosh!" I blurted.

Gran and Mama turned to look at me. "What?" they both asked at once.

I felt my cheeks starting to burn. "Um . . . nothing," I said.

Whatever had possessed me to tell Jake I could talk Gran into letting him use the carriage house? Those darn dimples of his must have addled my brain.

"Oh my, look at the time," said Gran. "Cecelia, dear, run in and turn the radio on. We'll be right in."

I groaned inwardly. How could I have forgotten about Gran's Sunday evening Jell-O program? The radio was one of the few modern inventions Gran actually liked, and she had her set programs that she had to listen to, come hell or high water. The Sunday night *Jell-O Hour* with Jack Benny was one of her favorites. I glanced out the kitchen window at the driveway. Maybe Jake had already found a place to stay. Or maybe he'd be late. "Take your time, Jake," I whispered under my breath.

"What's that?" asked Gran.

"Nothing. I was just . . . humming."

"Well, run along and turn the radio on like I asked, please."

"Yes, ma'am."

I walked into the front parlor to where our big mahogany console radio stood alongside the fireplace. I turned the knob, and after a bit of crackling and static, the sounds of Phil Harris's orchestra filled the room. Gran came in, untying her apron, and plopped down in her favorite chair with a satis-fied sigh. Mama followed and took her customary seat on the horsehair sofa.

I glanced out the parlor window at the gathering dusk. "Um, Gran," I said, "could I . . . uh . . . talk to you a second?"

"Can't it wait, Celie?" asked Gran. "Jack Benny's just coming on, and I'm in need of a good laugh."

"I suppose so," I said.

"Good," said Gran. "Have a seat, dear. You can use a laugh too." She looked pointedly at Mama. "We all can these days, can't we, Helen?"

Mama nodded shortly and fished her mending out of the basket by her feet. I perched on the other end of the sofa, keeping an uneasy eye out the window. No sooner had Jack Benny and Mary Livingston started their routine than I saw a yellow speck appear out of the dusk, moving steadily up the hill from town.

Please don't be Jake. Please don't be Jake, I chanted silently to myself. Who was I kidding? Who else in this county had a yellow car?

Gran threw her head back and laughed at one of Jack Benny's lines. "Did you hear that?" she said. "He just breaks me up, that man."

Despite my chanting, the yellow speck turned into an MG, and the MG turned into our driveway. As the rumbling of its engine grew louder, Gran and Mama looked up.

"Now who would that be this time of day?" asked Mama.

No way out but the truth now. "It's Jake-o-ob. Jacob Taylor. Um, I mean Mr. Taylor. The man from MDWSC."

Gran frowned. "What makes you think that?" she asked.

"Um . . . I recognize his car."

"Well, why on earth would he be coming out here on a Sunday night?" Gran mused, then she frowned. "I hope he doesn't think—"

"Ummm . . ." I interrupted. "I invited him."

"What?" asked Gran, squinting at me. "It sounded for a moment there like you said you *invited* him."

There was no backing down now, nothing to do but take the bull by the horns. I stood up. "I did," I said. "See, he needed a place to stay and every place in town was full up and they're tearing the hotel down and last night he had to sleep in his car. I met him downtown and he looked all tired and rumpled and I couldn't have him sleep in his car again—that wouldn't be neighborly, would it? You raised me to be neighborly, didn't you? And we have the empty room over the carriage house and he said he'd pay whatever you thought reasonable and besides, he's just doing his job. It's not his fault what's happening to the valley." I stopped to catch my breath, and glanced from Gran to Mama. "He's really very nice if you'd just give him a chance," I added apologetically.

I couldn't read Mama's face, but Gran was looking at me like I was Medusa and just the sight of me had frozen her with horror. Neither one of them said a word. Minutes dragged by as Jack Benny and Mary Livingston continued exchanging jokes in the background, then a knock came on the kitchen door. Gran's scowl deepened.

"I'll . . . get rid of him," I said with a sigh of resignation.

The knock came again, and I turned and fled from Gran's accusing stare, back through the house to the dusky kitchen.

I was about to say "I'm sorry" when I pulled the door open, but then there was Jacob Taylor smiling at me with those Clark Gable dimples, and next thing I knew I was opening the door wider and asking him in.

"How did it go with your grandmother?" he asked quietly.

"Um . . . could've been worse, I guess. I'm still alive."

Jake smiled. "I was afraid of that," he said. "Look, I'll just go. I really don't want to make any trouble."

The kitchen light clicked on and there was Mama, standing beneath it. "Good evening," she said.

Jake straightened. "Hello," he returned.

Mama came forward and offered her hand. "I'm Celie's mother," she said.

Jake's eyes widened. "Her mother!" he exclaimed. "You *can't* be her mother. You must be her sister. . . ."

Mama blushed and pulled her hand free. "You won't catch any flies with that kind of honey around here, Mister," she warned.

Jake blushed. "Sorry," he said, "but I meant it. Honestly. You just can't be that. . . ."

"*Old?*" I offered.

Jake looked at me with a stricken face, and Mama burst out laughing.

"All right, let's start this all over," she said, extending her hand again. "I'm Helen Wheeler, Cecelia's mother, and you are?"

"Jacob Taylor, ma'am," said Jake, shaking Mama's hand in a businesslike manner. "Pleased to make your acquaintance."

"Likewise," said Mama. She was still smiling broadly. "Celie tells us you're with the MDWSC."

"Yes, ma'am. I'm sorry about that. I know it's a dirty word around here, but—"

"Not to everyone," Mama interrupted. "And besides the point, it's your job, and a job is a precious thing in these hard times."

I looked at Mama in surprise. Was she taking my side against Gran?

"If it were up to me," she continued, "I'd be happy to rent you the room. But as you know, Mr. Taylor, the house belongs to my mother-in-law, and she can be rather. . . ."

"*Difficult?*"

We all turned to see Gran standing stiffly in the doorway. She looked at me and then at Mama. There was a pained look in her eyes. Betrayal? I wondered how much she had heard.

"Mrs. Wheeler," said Jake with a respectful dip of his head. "I'm sorry to have bothered you, ma'am. I truly am. And please don't be angry with your granddaughter. It was me that put her up to this. . . ."

"Oh hush," said Gran with an impatient toss of her head. "If there's one thing I know about my granddaughter, young man, it's that nobody puts her up to anythin' she doesn't want to be put up to. She comes by that naturally. She's a Wheeler."

"Yes, ma'am," said Jacob Taylor sheepishly. "Well, anyway, I'm sorry. I shouldn't have let her—"

"Aren't you listenin', young man?" Gran interrupted again. "That's the trouble with you young folks today, always talkin', never listening. What I'm sayin' is that you have nothing to apologize for. You didn't let my granddaughter do anything. She did exactly what she pleased and you are here because you were invited. Isn't that the truth?"

Jacob Taylor looked confused. "Well . . . yes, ma'am, I suppose it is."

"Good," said Gran. "I'm glad we got that settled. Now, the room'll be three dollars a week. There's a woodstove but no water. You can get what you need for cookin' and washin' from the pump in the barnyard, and you can use the old privy out back of the carriage house."

With that Gran turned and walked away, leaving the rest of us staring after her with our mouths agape.

14

Mama led the way with the lantern, a broom, and her feather duster. I followed, carrying sheets, blankets, and a pillow. Jake brought up the rear, lugging his valise. Inside the carriage house, Mama took another lantern down from a hook and lit it for Jake.

"There's no electricity out here," she said apologetically.

"Believe me, that's not a problem," said Jake. "I'm just obliged to have a roof over my head and someplace a little bigger than my car to stretch out in."

Mama nodded and proceeded to the foot of the staircase. She paused and pointed to the woodpile.

"You can help yourself to wood for the stove," she said, "but mind, be frugal. We've had no one to cut wood since we had to let Calvin go; we have to pay to have it brought in."

Let Calvin go? I looked at Mama in stunned surprise. I was always told that Calvin, our farmhand, left because he felt like "movin' on." I never heard anything about us letting him go. My mind jumped back to the day he left. I was only five years old, but I still remembered it clearly. He had taken me on his knee that afternoon and handed me a little matchbox full of nickels.

"I won't be here to take you to the candy store on payday no more, Missy," he said, "so you save these up, and each time your mama takes you to town, you buy a piece of candy and think of yer old friend Cal, okay?"

"Don't go, Calvin," I'd begged him, throwing my arms around his thick, bristly neck.

He had looked up at the trees for a long moment, then, in a husky voice said, "I got to go, Missy. I got to be movin' on."

I had grown angry and stubborn, and I'd refused to kiss him good-bye. I still remembered the deep sadness in his eyes as he picked up his satchel and walked away.

I stared at Mama in disbelief. Calvin was like a part of our family. How could she and Gran let him go? And why? Unless . . . I counted backward in my mind to the year I would have been five. *1929*. The year of the stock market crash. So . . . that was why. And that must have been why we sold off the farm animals and equipment and the bulk of the land too. The crash must have hit Gran hard.

"You should have told me," I said.

Mama looked at me blankly.

"You should have told me the truth about Calvin."

Mama blushed. "Celie, this isn't the time—"

"Why didn't you tell me?" I interrupted.

Mama flicked her eyes toward Jake and I knew what she was trying to say. This was family business, not to be aired in front of strangers. But I didn't care. I was angry and I wanted an answer.

"Why?" I repeated. "I deserved to know."

Mama gave an exasperated sigh. "You were too young to understand about the Depression," she said. "We didn't want to worry you."

"I would have understood," I said quietly, "better than I understood Calvin leaving us."

Mama glanced uncomfortably at Jake. "I'm sorry," she said. "You see, Calvin was like a father to Celie. Her own father died before she hardly knew him."

Jake shook his head sympathetically. "I'm sorry," he said to both of us.

"I never even kissed him good-bye," I mumbled.

"Your father?" asked Jake.

"No. *Calvin*." I glared at Mama.

"Hey." Jake bent his head close to mine. "You were just a little girl. Your mother and grandmother did what they thought best. No one meant to hurt you . . . or Calvin."

I looked into Jake's eyes for a long moment, and then I looked away. He was right, I knew. But still I wished I had known the truth. I wished I had kissed Cal good-bye.

Mama cleared her throat. "Well, come along, Mr. Taylor," she said. "We need to get you settled." She started up the stairs and Jake bowed to me and motioned me up ahead of him. With a sigh of resignation, I followed Mama. At the top of the stairs, she pushed the door open, and the stale smell of dust and mildew assaulted us. She hung her lantern on a hook just inside the door, and we stepped into the room. Jake carried his lantern in, too, and lifted it to have a look.

"Oh my," said Mama. "It *has* been a long time since anyone has been up here."

Cobwebs hung from the ceiling and drifted like snow across the window. Dust lay thick on the furniture and floor. Still, the room brought back warm memories for me. A pair of Calvin's old overalls dangled from a hook near the door, and one of his sweat-stained hats adorned a bedpost, tilting crookedly as if perched on a too-small head. In front of the window sat two wooden chairs and a small table, and on the table, still spread open, was an old game board. I walked over and gently wiped the dust away with my hand.

"Calvin and I used to play checkers on this," I said. "He's the one taught me how."

"Really?" said Jake. "You any good?"

I smiled. "Just try me."

Jake winked. "You're on."

Mama cleared her throat loudly. "First things first," she said, handing me the feather duster. "You start on the furniture, Celie, while I tackle these cobwebs."

"Oh no, please," Jake protested. "It's enough that you folks are putting me up this way. I can certainly do my own cleaning."

"Nonsense," said Mama. "We have nothing better to do tonight anyway, do we, Celie?"

"No, ma'am," I said eagerly. Mama usually quizzed me on vocabulary words on Sunday nights after the *Jell-O Hour*. I would have mucked out a barn full of horse manure to get out of that.

"If you want to help, though, you can haul that mattress downstairs and beat the dust out of it," Mama told Jake. "You'll find a rug beater hanging on the wall with the rest of the tools."

"Yes, ma'am." Jake saluted, then threw the mattress over his shoulder and headed for the stairs. Before long we heard the *whomp, whomp, whomp* of the rug beater.

"Celie," Mama said quietly, "have a care how friendly you are getting with this man. We hardly know him, after all. I don't want you up here alone with him, you understand?"

I frowned. "Why not? I used to come up here with Calvin."

"That was different," Mama said. "You were a little bitty girl then, and Calvin was like a member of the family. You're turning into a young woman now, and this fella is . . . well, he's. . . ."

"I *know* what he is, Mama," I said shortly. "And I can take care of myself just fine, thank you."

Mama gave me a little smirk. "Just the same," she said, "if there's any checker playing to be done, it's to be done down in the main house."

I grimaced, and Mama raised her eyebrows. "You hear me, Celie Wheeler?" she asked.

"Yes, ma'am," I grumbled. "I'm not *deaf*."

After a time the whomping stopped and Jake reappeared in the doorway with the mattress slung over his back. Mama had all the cobwebs down and I was making short work of the dust. Jake put the mattress back on the bed and Mama bustled about making it up while Jake took the broom to the floor.

"There," said Mama, when we were all done. "That'll do for tonight. Tomorrow we'll wash those windows up and scrub the floor and the place'll be good as new."

"You're really too kind," Jake protested.

"Nonsense," Mama said once again. "Just common hospitality." She motioned to me. "Come along, Celie. I'm sure Mr. Taylor can use a good night's sleep."

"I'd be obliged if you'd all call me by my first name," Jake said as he followed us to the door.

Mama stopped and looked back. "I'm afraid we don't know you well enough, Mr. Taylor," she said. "I don't think it wise to rush into familiarity, do you?"

"No, ma'am," said Jake. "I'm sorry." But when Mama turned her back again, he gave me a wink.

I smiled. Jake thought Mama was old-fashioned. But we were young and modern, he and I. A little shiver of delight coursed through my body. Jake Taylor, with his Clark Gable dimples, was actually going to be living in our carriage house!

15

I awoke to a sharp whacking sound and hopped out of bed to investigate.

"What's that racket?" asked Gran as she shuffled out of her room, knotting her robe.

I ran the length of the upstairs hall and peered out the back window.

"It's J— Mr. Taylor," I said. "He's splitting those logs that have been stacked alongside the carriage house ever since the last nor'easter."

Although Gran tried to look tight-lipped and stern, I could tell that she was pleased. Industry was a quality she had always admired.

"He might've waited till the house was awake," she grumbled as she started for the stairs.

I turned my attention back to the window. Jake was wearing Calvin's old overalls without a shirt, and the morning sun glinted off the sweat on his bare arms. The muscles of his chest and upper arms bulged in a most pleasing way as he swung the ax.

"What are you looking at, Cecelia?" Mama asked as she padded out of her room in her robe and slippers.

"Nothing," I said, blushing as she came up behind me. "Just Mr. Taylor chopping wood. He's right handy with an ax."

Mama looked over my shoulder. "Hmmm," she said appreciatively, "so he is." We watched together for a moment. "A might chilly to be out without a shirt, don't you think?" Mama said.

"Not if you're working hard, I don't suppose."

"Mmmm," said Mama.

As if he sensed our eyes upon him, Jake suddenly paused midswing and looked directly up at us. Mama and I both jumped back from the window as though we'd been caught peeking through a knothole in the privy. Then we looked at each other and burst out giggling.

"Just look at us," said Mama, "acting so silly. What's the harm in watching a man chop wood?"

"None," I said with a shrug. But then we both giggled again.

"Go on," said Mama, giving me a playful tap on the rear. "Get ready for school."

"I'm not going," I reminded her. "Gran wants me to go with you to the cemetery."

Mama's smile faded. "Oh, that's right," she said quietly. "How could I have forgotten?"

"Do I have to go, Mama?" I asked. "I don't like cemeteries."

"Nobody likes cemeteries, Celie," Mama said. "Gran and I haven't asked you to go to any of the other disinterments, but we think it's fitting that you be at your father's. Go along now, and put on something dark and respectful."

"Yes, ma'am," I mumbled. I went back to my room and put on a navy blue blouse and dark blue and green plaid skirt, then I dragged down to breakfast. Gran set out some oatmeal for me, then headed back upstairs to get herself dressed. I toyed with the oatmeal, dreading the day's events.

Mama came down wearing her funeral clothes, a black shirtwaist dress and a little black hat with a small veil that came down over her eyes. She scooped some oatmeal out of the pot on the back of the stove, poured herself a cup of tea, and sat down beside me.

"I'll be glad when this is over," she said with a sigh. "I'll be glad when it's *all* over." She fiddled with the spoon in her tea. "Have you given any more thought to moving, Celie?" she asked quietly.

I swallowed my mouthful of oatmeal with difficulty. "Sort of," I said.

"And?"

"And . . . Well, Chubby's father is buying a filling station in Warton, and some of my other friends are moving there, too, and I thought. . . ."

"Warton?" Mama said the word like it meant *dung.*

"Yes," I hurried on. "Warton has a picture show, and a department store too."

Mama snorted. "If you can call it that. Warton is nothing but a dried-up old mill town, Celie. It's dying just like this valley."

"There are some nice parts," I insisted. "Out by Sandy Pond is nice. We could maybe even find a modern little house."

Mama closed her eyes and rubbed them wearily. "Never mind," she said. "I shouldn't have brought it up. I haven't the energy to deal with this today."

Gran walked back into the kitchen in her black funeral dress. It hung loosely, and I was startled to see how thin she had become just since a few weeks ago when I last saw her in it.

"Did you eat breakfast yet, Gran?" I asked.

"Haven't any appetite," Gran said as she pinned her hat on her head. An engine started up outside, and she turned to look out the window. "Celie," she said suddenly, "run out and tell that young man I want a word with him."

I groaned inwardly. "You're not going to yell at him about waking us up, are you?" I asked. "I'm sure he was only trying to be helpful."

"Never you mind what I'm a-goin' to do," said Gran. "Just tell him to come in here, please."

I sighed and trudged out to the porch to flag down the MG.

"Hey there!" said Jake cheerfully. "Don't you look pretty this morning."

My heart fluttered. Could Jake Taylor possibly think I was pretty, or was he just teasing me? He looked well rested and clean-shaven and his eyes were as blue as the morning sky.

"Is there something I can do for you?" Jake asked.

"Oh." I realized I'd been staring. "Sorry. Yes. My grandmother would like to speak to you."

Jake cringed. "She isn't throwing me out already, is she?"

I shrugged helplessly. "I hope not."

Jake turned off his engine and hopped out of the MG. "Well, might as well face the music," he said. He followed me back into the kitchen. "Morning, Mrs. Wheeler, Mrs. Wheeler," he said with a nod first to Mama, then to Gran. "What can I do for you?"

"Set and have some breakfast," said Gran.

"Oh, I couldn't—"

"*Set.*"

"Yes, ma'am."

Jake sat down and Gran scooped him up a bowl of oatmeal. "Mind you eat it quickly," Gran said. "The car will be by shortly."

"The car?" said Jake.

"To take us to the cemetery," said Gran.

"Oh, yes." Jake nodded. "Don't you worry. I won't hold you up." He shoveled a heaping spoon of oatmeal into his mouth.

"You won't be holdin' us up," said Gran. "You'll be comin' with us."

Jake looked up with bulging cheeks. He swallowed hard. "Coming with you?" he repeated. He glanced at Mama and me, but we were as much in the dark as he was. "Well . . . uh . . . thank you, Mrs. Wheeler," he stammered with a look of pure puzzlement on his face, "but . . . I'm afraid I've got to get to my job."

"I thought *I* was your job," said Gran.

Jake shrugged. "Well, yes, ma'am, you are . . . part of it, but—"

"Then you'll do my part of it this mornin'," said Gran. "If a man takes on a job, he ought to know the whole of what it is he's doin'. Won't take but a coupl'a hours."

Jake glanced helplessly at Mama and me again, then he nodded reluctantly. "All right then," he said to Gran.

16

The idea of having Jake along made the prospect of the whole cemetery business seem a little less bleak. There'd be someone cheery to talk to at least, not to mention someone nice to look at. When the funeral car arrived, Jake opened both of the side doors and helped Gran climb into the big backseat. Before anyone could say a word, I slid into the middle seat. Then, to my great displeasure, Mama slid in beside me.

"Aren't you going to sit in the back with Gran?" I asked.

"No," she said. "Why?"

"Never mind," I huffed as Jake walked around and got into the front seat with the driver. The funeral car pulled out of our driveway and turned toward town. A short distance up the road we saw Aunt Stella standing at the end of her driveway, dressed in black and clutching her purse in front of her ample bosom. She waved for the car to stop and opened Gran's door.

"I thought you could use some comp'ny this mornin'," she said to Gran.

Gran's eyes grew shiny. She opened her mouth as if to speak, but no words come out. She looked down at her lap, and Aunt Stella climbed in beside her and gently patted her hand.

"Go ahead," Aunt Stella called to the driver.

We got held up by the construction in the center of town and had to watch as the demolition team swarmed over the Swift River Hotel. Aunt Stella clucked her tongue.

"What a pity," she said. "We had some good times there, didn't we, Lizzie?"

Gran nodded silently.

Aunt Stella chuckled to herself, as if remembering some private joke.

"What's so funny, Aunt Stella?" I asked.

"I was just rememberin' the time the Swift River Hotel got struck by lightnin'," she said. "The Congregational pastor told the owner, Bill Galbin, that it was a sign that God considered the Hotel an evil place. Well, don't you know, the church steeple got struck a few weeks later and Bill turned 'round and told the pastor that same thing."

We all laughed. It felt good to laugh. Aunt Stella always was a good one for livening up a somber situation.

The traffic started to move again and the pit in my stomach returned as we made our way up Hill Street to the cemetery gates. The old cemetery, once rolling and green, was barren and desolate now. Most of the graves had already been moved and only a few lonely-looking headstones remained. As we drew near our family plot, I could see that the graves of my father and my baby aunt were already open. The driver pulled the car over, and he and Jake came around to help us out. The sky had clouded over and a chill breeze had come up. I shivered, partly from the cold, partly from the dread of seeing what waited within those open graves. Mama took one of Gran's arms and Aunt Stella took the other. I trailed behind.

The ground was muddied and torn from all the excavations, and our shoes sank as we walked. Two crows jeered at us from the branches of a big old oak, calling shrilly to each other, as if making rude comments. Workmen waited on either side of the two open holes, holding ropes, ready to lift the caskets when Gran gave the okay.

Mama and Gran and Aunt Stella walked up to the graves and Gran looked down, first into one hole, then the other. She nodded and the men began to pull on the ropes. Two dirt-crusted caskets rose slowly out of the ground, one tiny, one large. Gooseflesh prickled on my arms at the thought of my father's body lying there within that box. Oddly, though, I found myself even more saddened by the little casket that held the aunt I'd never known. I hadn't expected it to be so small. How hard it must have been for Gran to lay that little child in the ground.

I looked at Gran, standing between the two caskets, childlike herself in her overlarge dress. She seemed too frail to have withstood all the tragedy that life had dealt her, but she was not frail, I knew. She was strong . . . as strong as the oak that towered over our heads. At least she always had been. As she turned and started walking back toward me, I was struck by how old and tired she suddenly appeared. She leaned heavily on Mama and Aunt Stella. I could see pain in all their faces, tears in all their eyes. Tears sprang to mine, too, and my heart ached, not for the two strangers sleeping in the caskets but for the pain of these women who were left behind, these women that I loved so much. I turned and walked with them back to the car where Jake and the driver waited. Gran stopped at the car door and turned back for a last look at the cemetery.

"When I was a little girl," she said in a faltering voice, "there was an old Indian who used to come here each spring. He'd sit all day, chanting some kind of prayer, and tears would run down his cheeks. I remember wonderin' if he wept for the loss of a loved one or the loss of his land. Now I know they were one 'n the same." She turned to look at Jake. "You can take our bodies out of this valley, Mr. Taylor," she said, "but you'll never take our souls. When you flood this land you'll be drownin' a part of us, just as sure as if you took our heads and pushed 'em down under that water."

Quabbin Park Cemetery was a beautiful place, vast and green, and carefully tended. We lay my father and baby aunt in the plot beside my grandfather. The older generations of Wheelers were there, too, their headstones dating back hundreds of years. Gran stood silently, staring at their many graves. Aunt Stella was still at her arm, but Mama had gone over to speak with Mr. Potter, the undertaker.

I walked up and slipped my hand into Gran's. Her skin was waxy and thin, and I could feel her delicate bones beneath it. For so many years I had been the child and she the caretaker. Now it seemed as though our roles had slowly begun to change. I tried to find some comforting words for her.

"It's pretty here, Gran," I said. "I think Daddy would like it if he could see it. I think the others would too."

Gran said nothing. She was no longer crying, but she seemed beaten down by sadness. I wanted to take the burden from her. I wanted to make her smile again.

And then I saw Mama. She had finished her conversation with the undertaker and was standing alone and silent beside my father's casket. She seemed to be staring through it, beyond it, at something I couldn't see. Slowly she reached out and touched the lid, then her whole body shuddered as a sob escaped her lips. Tears sprang anew to my eyes, and I rushed to her side. She turned and folded me in her arms and we clung to each another, quietly crying together.

This wasn't fair, I thought. No one had a right to open up these old wounds, to make Mama and Gran hurt like this all over again. As we walked back toward the car, I saw Jake watching us and my anger erupted.

"I hope you're happy," I snapped at him. "And I hope all those greedy people back in Boston drown in their stupid water!"

17

The silence was heavy in the car on the way home. At last Jake turned to us and cleared his throat.

"I . . . I know this doesn't help much," he said, "but I'm really sorry you people have to go through all this."

No one answered.

"I'd . . . uh . . . like to take you all out for some dinner if you'd allow me," he went on. "Do you have a favorite restaurant nearby?"

"Not anymore," I snapped.

Aunt Stella sighed heavily. "Now, Celie, mind your manners," she said. "It doesn't make any sense to take our bad feelings out on Mr. Taylor. Land sakes, he was prob'ly still messin' his diapers when this whole project got under way."

Jake turned scarlet, and I couldn't help but giggle.

"I've got dinner waitin' on the stove for all of us," Aunt Stella continued. "I'd be obliged if you'd join us, Mr. Taylor. I always do enjoy having a man to feed, specially one as easy on the eyes as you."

"Stella Bancroft!" Gran cried. "I declare!"

Stella threw her head back and laughed. "Well, it's the truth," she said. "I'm not dead yet. I still like to look."

Jake laughed and Stella gave him a wink, then lowered her voice in a mock attempt at confidentiality. "My own poor excuse for a husband ran off years ago with some little floozy from up Atkinson Hollow way," she told him.

Jake winked back. "Man must've been a fool," he said.

"Stella," Gran scolded, "how many times have I told you not to go around airing your dirty laundry in front of strangers."

Stella gave out one of her hearty, bosom-shaking laughs. "About as many times as I've told you to loosen up that corset of yours a notch or two, dear," she replied.

Gran snorted and I smiled, happy to see the people in my life acting like themselves again.

"Surely you folks had opportunities to be heard before this project went forward," Jake said as we sat around Aunt Stella's dining room table, sipping our tea and finishing up our rhubarb pie.

Gran gave a short laugh. "Oh yes," she said, "we had opportunities all right—long as we could get to the hearings, which were *conveniently* held in Boston."

Boston. I scowled. I had come to hate that town. I'd never been there, didn't even know anyone there, but I hated it. In my mind it had assumed the shape of a great, thirsty beast intent on devouring our little valley.

"Do you know what it took to get to Boston from here back in the early twenties, Mr. Taylor?" Gran asked.

"No, ma'am," said Jake. "I don't guess I do."

"Well," said Gran, with a self-satisfied smile, "I'm fixin' to tell you. You could take the train, of course, but the train didn't go direct from the valley to Boston. So, if you wanted to get to Boston for a ten o'clock hearing, say, you had to catch an afternoon train to Athol or Springfield, spend the night, then catch the train to Boston first thing in the mornin'. Once the hearing was over, you could catch the afternoon train back to Athol or Springfield, but you had to wait till the next day to get a train back to the valley. For the menfolk that often meant three days away from work. Mind you—they didn't hold those things on weekends. How many of us do you think could afford that kind of trip every time there was a hearing?"

"Not many, I s'pose," said Jake, "but why couldn't you drive? There were cars back then."

"Oh sure," said Gran. "There were cars. But again, if you wanted to be in Boston for a mornin' hearing, you'd better go up the day before because most of the roads were just dirt then, and car tires weren't what they are today. You had to figure on changing anywhere from one to ten flat tires on a trip to Boston and back. And there weren't any fillin' stations back then, either. You had to change your own tires, and you had to carry your own gas, or go out of your way to find a general store 'twixt here and there that carried the stuff."

"The simple truth is, we got this reservoir rammed down our throats, Mr. Taylor," Stella put in. "Boston gets what Boston wants. That's always been the way of it out here in the west, and I guess it always will be."

I sniffed. "It's not fair," I said. "I'd like to see what would happen if somebody tried to take Boston and make a reservoir out of it."

Jake laughed. "That *would* be something to see." Then he shook his head. "But word back in Boston was that most folks out here welcomed this project. We heard that the valley had been dying for years, and that the majority were glad of a way out, a chance to make a new start."

"There's some truth in that," Mama confirmed, "but you've got to remember that it was the rumors about the dam that killed the valley. Soon as they started, way back around the turn of the century, property values fell. Folks quit moving in, businesses started moving out. By the time the Swift River Act was finally passed, a lot of folks were in pretty desperate straits, stuck here jobless in houses worth less than the mortgages they owed. And then, on top of all that, the Depression hit."

Jake stared grimly into his teacup. "No wonder you folks hate the whole business," he said quietly.

"*Hate* is a strong word, Mr. Taylor," Aunt Stella said. "Most of us are old Yankee pragmatists, out this way. We know enough to accept what we can't change. We had us a real nice bone out here, and a bigger dog wanted it. We have to accept that. But we don't have to like it."

Jake nodded. "Have you made plans yet, Mrs. Bancroft?" he asked.

Aunt Stella drew in a deep breath and let it out slowly. "Matter of fact," she said quietly, "I just took me a room in a home up in Athol."

Gran's teacup clattered into her saucer, sloshing tea all over Aunt Stella's lace tablecloth. "A home!" she cried. "What kind of a home?"

Aunt Stella stiffened her back like a dog bracing for a fight. "An old folks' home, of course," she stated.

"An old folks' home!" Gran threw her hands up in the air. "Now I've heard ever'thing. You no more b'long in an old folks' home than Celie does, Stella."

"Now don't you be tellin' me my business," Aunt Stella argued. "I'm seventy-eight years old and I'm not about to go through the folderol of buying a house or settin' up an apartment just to have to move all over again when my health starts goin' downhill a year or two down the road."

"Well, I won't have you goin' to a home, I can tell you that!" declared Gran. "Settin' in a rocking chair all day long, discussin' who's sick and who's dyin'. . . . Next thing you know you're shufflin' and droolin'."

Aunt Stella laughed. "Well, it's a free country," she said. "I can shuffle and drool if I've a mind to."

Gran snorted. "Horsefeathers!" she said. "You'll come live with me, and that's the end of it."

"Come live with you where?" asked Aunt Stella.

We all turned to Gran at once, hanging on her answer.

"Why in one of the empty bedrooms, of course," she said. "Lord knows we have enough of them."

Mama let out an exasperated sigh, and Jake and Aunt Stella and I all exchanged glances.

"Gran," said Mama.

Gran ignored her.

"Gran," Mama repeated emphatically. "*We* have to move too."

Gran put her napkin on the table. "Maybe not," she said.

"What?" said Mama.

We all stared at Gran open mouthed.

"Have you got some miracle up your sleeve?" Mama asked.

Gran looked at Jake and lifted her chin. "Mr. Taylor," she said. "I have a proposition for you."

Jake's brow furrowed. "Don't know that I can help any," he said, "but go ahead."

Gran nodded. "I'm an old woman," she continued. "Stella here is an old woman, too, and there's a handful of others left in town, jest as old as we are. I've got a big house, Mr. Taylor, with lots of empty rooms—plenty enough for all of us that's left. How much can one house hurt this watershed thing you folks talk about? B'fore long we'll all be dead. Then you can tear the house down and be done with us. Jest . . ." Gran's voice broke and tears stood in her eyes. "Jest please . . . let us die here, in our valley."

My throat felt like I'd swallowed a knife. So this was what Gran had up her sleeve—why she'd let Jake move into the carriage house, why she'd dragged him to the cemetery this afternoon. It hurt me to see her so desperate, to hear my proud, strong grandmother beg.

Jake shook his head slowly. "I'm sorry, Mrs. Wheeler," he said, "but . . . I don't have any power with the commission. And even if I did . . . Do you know how many people have asked for exceptions? We can't do for one and not for others. The law is the law. It has to apply to everyone just the same."

Gran looked down at the table and blinked a few times, then she sniffed. "Well, Stella, that was a real nice meal," she said. "Let me give you a hand washing up these dishes."

"Gran," Mama said quietly. "Mr. Taylor is right. The law is the law, and I think it's time you accepted it and signed the papers."

Gran got up and started clearing dishes as though she hadn't heard Mama say a word.

"*Gran*," said Mama, more loudly.

Stella reached over and touched Mama's hand, but Mama shook her head. "No, Stella," she said. "We can't go on like this. She's got to face facts."

"Mama," I interrupted, "maybe now's not a good—"

Mama looked at me sharply. "Celie," she said, "why don't you run along to school? You'll still be in time for the afternoon session."

I was about to protest when Jake cleared his throat. "I'd be happy to drive her in, Mrs. Wheeler," he said, rising from his seat. "I'm on my way into town anyway."

"That's very kind," said Mama. "I'm sure Celie would be pleased to accept a ride." She turned to me for confirmation.

For a brief moment I was torn, wanting to stay and eavesdrop on the conversation between Mama and Gran and Aunt Stella, but the thought of a ride in Jake's convertible was just too tempting.

"Sure," I said. "That'd be swell."

18

The chill wind whipped my hair around my face and brought tears to my eyes.

"You sure this isn't too much for you?" Jake shouted.

"No sir!" I yelled. Jake had wanted to put the top up before we left home, but I would have none of it. I'd always dreamed of riding in a convertible, and I wasn't about to let a little unpleasant weather stop me. "This is the *berries*!" I cried.

Jake laughed. "Glad you like it," he said. "Little cold today for my blood."

I looked over at Jake with his sparkling eyes and rosy cheeks and his golden hair flying in the wind, and my heart swelled. For a moment I let myself daydream about how it would feel to be his girl. Wouldn't Belinda Wilder turn green! I looked down at Jake's hand resting lightly on the stick shift. Ever so casually, I allowed mine to sort of slip off the seat until it brushed, just lightly, against his.

Jake glanced at me, then down at my hand. I pulled it back.

"Everything okay?" he asked.

"Yes," I said, blushing.

"You want to try shifting?" he asked.

My mouth dropped. "And how!" I shouted. "Can I?"

"Sure," said Jake. "Give me your hand."

Jake slowed the car to a stop, then he put my hand on the shift, covering it with his own. My skin tingled at his touch.

"This is first," he said, "then over and up to second, then all the way forward is third. You ready?"

"Yes," I said, feeling a bit light-headed.

"Okay. Put her in first."

I did as Jake said, then he slowly let out the clutch and we lurched forward.

"Great," he said. "Now listen to the engine. Hear it starting to rev? That means it's ready to go into second. When I step on the clutch, you do it just like I showed you."

Jake put the clutch in, and I slid the shift into second gear.

"Look at that!" said Jake. "Smooth as silk. Okay, listen again and tell me when you think it's ready for third."

I listened carefully as the engine wound up.

"Now?" I asked.

Jake grinned. "You're a natural, young lady," he said as we shifted into third. "There. That's it. What a team, eh?" He squeezed my hand, and for a moment I could hardly catch my breath. Was it just me, or was Jake acting more than friendly? Could he possibly be feeling toward me the way I was feeling toward him? My heart quickened at the thought.

"I . . . I'm not in any real hurry to get to school," I stammered. "We could drive around some more if you'd like."

Jake laughed. "That *would* be fun," he said, "but I'm afraid I've got to get to the office."

"Oh."

"But don't you worry," Jake said and gave me a wink, "I'm going to take you out for a real ride first chance I get."

"Really?"

"Sure," said Jake. "I'll be looking forward to it."

We passed the town hall, all draped with red, white, and blue bunting for Wednesday night's ball. Suddenly I had the most wonderful idea!

"Say," I said, "are you busy Wednesday night?"

"Busy?" Jake shook his head. "Don't think so. Why?"

"Well, there's going to be a ball," I said, "an old-fashioned Fireman's Ball, only this one is *really* special because it's going to be the last one ever. They're holding it on Wednesday because on that night at midnight Enfield ceases to be a town."

Jake nodded. "Mmm," he said. "I heard about that. Sounds like kind of a sad occasion."

I shrugged. "I think that's partly why they're having it," I said. "To try to cheer everybody up. There's going to be a concert and dancing, and lots of food and everything!"

"I suppose that *is* a good way for the town to go out," Jake agreed.

I nodded. "And the thing is," I continued, "we have an extra ticket because Mama bought herself one and then Tom Kessler went and bought her one too."

"I see," said Jake, beginning to smile.

"And so I was wondering if . . . maybe if you weren't too busy or anything, maybe you'd like to go?"

Jake threw his head back and laughed, then he looked at

me and grinned. "Why, Miss Celie Wheeler," he said, "are you asking me out on a date?"

I grinned too. "I guess I am," I admitted.

"Well, that is a first," said Jake. "I don't believe I've ever been asked out by a young lady before."

"Well, that makes two firsts, then," I said, "because I never asked a man out before, either."

Jake laughed. "Well, I am honored to be the first," he said, "and I'd be pleased to escort you to the ball."

"Copacetic!" I shouted.

To my utter delight, my class was still out at lunch recess when we arrived at school. I asked Jake to pull up and drop me off right in front of the schoolyard.

"Good-bye," I called out loudly as he pulled away. "I'll be looking forward to our date!"

Jake gave a little farewell toot on his horn, then zoomed away. I couldn't hide my grin as I entered the schoolyard. Belinda came running over.

"Who was *that?*" she asked.

Leaning against the fence a few feet away, pretending to be reading a book but taking in every word, was Chubby.

"He's just a fella that's staying with us out at the house," I said smugly.

Chubby's head swiveled.

"Oooh!" Belinda shrieked. "You are s-o-o lucky! Why is he staying with you? How old is he? Where did he get that car."

"He's from the MDWSC," I said, "and we're renting him a room. He's twenty-four, and he's taking me to the ball on Wednesday. I'll introduce you if you'd like."

Belinda's eyes flew wide. "You're full of applesauce!" she shrieked. "That sheik is *not* taking you to the ball!"

I smiled serenely. "Wait till Wednesday," I said, "and see for yourself."

Miss Rourke came out onto the schoolhouse steps and rang her bell.

"I just can't believe it. You're s-o-o lucky," Belinda repeated as she hurried off to gather up her lunch pail. Chubby folded his book and started to walk away.

"Hey," I said. "Wait up."

He turned to look at me coolly but said nothing.

I ran a step to catch up with him.

"What's eating you?" I asked.

"Nothin'," he said sullenly.

"You still mad at me over what I said at the lake?" I asked.

Chubby shrugged.

"Okay, I'm sorry," I said. "I didn't mean it like it sounded. I know you're a real boy."

"Thanks," said Chubby flatly.

"Oh c'mon," I said. "Don't be such a goof. Did you see Jake's car? Isn't it the keenest? Maybe I can get him to give you a ride sometime."

Chubby snorted. "Don't do me any favors," he said.

I stopped and put my hands on my hips. "Will you get off your high hat?" I said. "What's got into you anyway?"

Chubby frowned. "I don't trust that guy," he said. "He looks like a lounge lizard to me, driving around in that struggle buggy of his with a girl half his age. He'd better not try anything with you or I'll. . . ."

I rolled my eyes. "Chubby Miller, you're all wet," I insisted. "Jake is a complete gentleman, and even if he wasn't, I'm no dumb Dora. I don't need you to play big brother."

"Fine," said Chubby. "Just don't come crying on my

shoulder when he drops you for the first hot number that comes along."

I twirled the end of my braid slowly around my finger and smiled. "Why, Chubby Miller," I teased, "I do believe you're jealous."

Chubby flushed bright red. "Go fly a kite," he snapped.

19

I burst through the door after school, eager to tell all about my ride in Jake's car and how Belinda was so jealous, but my excitement faded when I saw Mama. She was sitting alone at the kitchen table, reading the paper, and when she looked up, her eyes were troubled. The house seemed unusually quiet.

"Where's Gran?" I asked.

"She went for a walk."

"Is something wrong?"

Mama sighed. "We had words," she said. "I told her she's being selfish and pigheaded about this whole moving affair."

I was quiet for a moment, trying to gauge the seriousness of the situation. "Was she . . . really mad?" I asked.

Mama nodded.

I pulled out a chair and sat down heavily. Ginger came running and I scooped her up onto my lap. I could tolerate almost anything—anything but Gran and Mama fighting.

They bickered a lot, and now and then they had one of their "discussions," but once or twice in the past they had had serious clashes, and when they did, it felt as if the earth were shaking beneath my feet.

Mama rubbed her eyes tiredly. "I'm at my wits end with her, Celie," she said. "She just won't listen to reason. She won't *listen* at all. And time's running out. If we don't make plans, they'll be putting us out on the street with nothing more than what we can carry in a sack."

I lifted Ginger up and buried my face in her neck.

"I was thinking," Mama continued, "maybe you could talk some sense into her. You're the person she loves most in the world. Maybe she'll listen to you."

I looked up at Mama. "But . . . I don't want to make her mad at *me*," I protested.

Mama shook her head. "She never gets mad at you," she said. "Not really. She may fuss and grumble sometimes, but she loves you to death, and she can't stay angry at you for more than five minutes put together."

I sighed. "What do you want me to tell her?"

"That we have to make plans," Mama said. "That maybe . . . maybe it's time we all made a fresh start, moved somewhere far away from all this."

My heart sank. I stared at a worn spot on the oilcloth table cover until it blurred into nothingness.

"Celie?" said Mama.

I slowly shook my head. "I can't tell her that," I said. "Gran's too old to make a fresh start. Her whole life, all her memories, everything she loves is in this valley. If you take her far away from it, she won't even know who she is."

Mama fell silent.

"What's wrong?" I asked.

"You're right," she said quietly. She got up and walked to the kitchen sink. She rested her hands on the rim and stared out the window. Her back was to me, but I could tell she was crying.

"Mama?" I said.

She dabbed at her eyes with a kitchen towel, sniffed, and then took a deep breath. When she turned to me again she was smiling, but the smile was so thin I could see right through it. "I don't suppose Warton will be so bad," she said bravely. "It has a picture show anyway. We'll get to see *Gone with the Wind* one of these years."

I smiled doubtfully. "Are you sure, Mama? Do you think you could be happy there?"

Mama shrugged. "Why not? I suppose one place is as good as another when you come right down to it. I'll go downtown tomorrow and see if I can find some information on what kind of property's available over there."

My heart leaped. "You mean it?"

Mama smiled. "I'll look into it," she said. "Can't promise we're going to find anything suitable."

I flew out of my chair, and Ginger landed with a thump on the floor and yowled indignantly. I threw my arms around Mama's waist. "We *will* find something," I insisted. "I know we will. Oh, thank you, Mama. I can't wait to tell Gran!"

"Whoa there," Mama said. "Don't go putting the cart before the horse. You let me do some investigating and get my ducks in a row before we bring this up to Gran."

"Okay," I said. "I'll wait. But can I go look for her at least and tell her you're not mad anymore?"

Mama laughed. "Yes," she said with a slow nod of her head.

"You can do that." There was an unmistakable note of resignation in her voice, and I knew she wasn't really happy about
giving up her dream. But nobody was really happy about the
situation, I convinced myself. Gran wanted to stay right here
in Enfield. Mama wanted to move far away. It was only fitting
that both of them should settle for something in between,
especially if it meant we could stay close to the valley—and
Chubby.

20

I found Gran in the carriage house, sitting silently in the back of our old horse-drawn sleigh.

"What are you doin', Gran?" I asked.

"Rememberin'," she said, a faint smile on her lips. She ran her hand fondly along the worn sideboard of the sleigh. "Oh, we had some good times in the old days, Celie. Your grandfather proposed to me in this sleigh, y'know."

I climbed up and sat down beside her, and she reached an arm around me and pulled me close. I lay my head on her shoulder, snuggling in for a story. "Tell me, Gran," I said.

"It was back in eighty-five. I was but nineteen," she began, then she shook her head and clicked her tongue. "My lands . . . was I ever that young?"

"Go on, Gran," I prodded.

"It was about a week b'fore Christmas," she continued, "and we were out for an old-fashioned sleigh ride—your granddaddy and I, and Stuart Franklin—you know the

Franklins—they used to run that feed store over to Smith's Village?"

I nodded.

"And, let's see. There was Mary Hastings from over on Blue Meadow. Stuart was her beau. And then there was Belle Martin—her daddy ran the 'pothecary back then—and her beau was . . ."

"Gr-a-n," I said. "Are you going to tell me everyone's life history?"

Gran laughed. "Well, anyhow," she said, "we were with a group of the young folks we used to pal around with back then. It had snowed early in the day, and the night was icy cold, but we were warm as toast, the sleigh heaped high with straw, and plenty of robes and blankets piled on. We even had hot pieces of soapstone wrapped in flannel to keep our feet warm. Not that we needed 'em. We were warm as toast just holdin' each other's hands back then."

Gran gave me a wink, and I laughed. "How could you see where you were going in the dark?" I asked.

"We used to hang lanterns over the side, but we hardly needed 'em that night—the moon was so bright." Gran looked up toward the ceiling, and I knew that she was no longer seeing the old rafters above us. Instead she was back beneath the starlit sky of that long-ago night.

"I can still hear the clip-clop of the horses' hooves and see their white breath pourin' out like steam," she went on. "And the jingle of the harness bells. Is there another sound in the world as merry as the jinglin' of sleigh bells? My how we laughed and sang as we glided along sleek as silver over the snow."

"Where were you going?" I asked.

"To a dance over to the Swift River Hotel. I wish you could have seen it that night, Celie. It was lit up like a palace, the golden glow of the gaslights shinin' out through the windows, guiding us in. Other sleighs were comin' in from near and far, and we were all in high spirits, shouting and calling greetings to one another. When we pulled up out front we could hear the fiddle music from inside, and didn't it make our blood race? We crowded through the doors and watched as the dancers whirled around the floor in a reel. The stomp, stomp, stomp of their shoes on the old wooden floorboards soon had our toes tapping. Next thing we all joined in, reelin' and stompin' the night away."

"Sounds like fun," I said.

"Oh, it 'twas," said Gran softly, "'twas. We danced till almost midnight, didn't set down once. Then the hotel put out coffee and sandwiches to fortify us for the ride home. And we relished them, I'll tell you! All that reelin' and stompin' gives a body an appetite."

"So when did Grandfather propose?" I asked.

"Hold your horses," said Gran with a laugh. "I'm gettin' round to it. Well, much as we hated to see the evenin' end, comes a time when you've got to go home. We piled back into the sleigh—and I didn't know it, of course—but your grandfather had told his driver to go the long way around and drop everyone else off before me. After we'd made the rounds of the houses and the others had all said their good-byes, your grandfather pulled me close and asked me if he could give me a kiss."

"He asked you?" I said. "Why didn't he just do it?"

Gran sniffed. "Because he was a gentleman, of course, and gentlemen *ask*."

"And did you say yes?"

"What do you think?" Gran grinned.

I giggled. "I think you did."

Gran giggled too. "Oh yes," she said. "Yes, yes, yes! He was so handsome he took my breath away."

I thought of Jake and sighed. "Then what?" I asked.

"Then he reached into his vest pocket and pulled out a ring. 'Elizabeth,' he said. 'These last many months shared with you have been the happiest of my life. I can think of no greater joy than having you by my side always. Would you do me the honor of becoming my wife?'"

Gran's voice broke and she quickly wiped a tear from her cheek.

I hugged her tight. "That's so beautiful, Gran," I whispered.

"Mmmm," she said, rubbing my back, then she sighed. "He died when I was forty-seven, too young to be a widow, but we had twenty-eight wonderful years together, and I am grateful for that."

"And that's why I've decided to give you and your mother the money from the sale of the house and move with Stella to the old folks' home."

I pulled back. "*What?*"

Gran straightened, her jaw jutting out in that don't-argue-with-me-my mind's-made-up way.

"No, Gran," I said. "Mama has decided to stay. She's going downtown tomorrow to see about finding us a house in Warton."

"Horsefeathers," said Gran. "Your mama has been stuck out here in the sticks long enough. It's time she got on with livin'."

I shook my head and started to protest again, but Gran shushed me.

"You listen to me now, Celie," she said. "Your mama was widowed at twenty-one. Twenty-one! She was hardly more than a child herself, left alone in this big old ark of a house with a little baby and a crotchety old woman for her sole companions. For a time it worked all right. I needed her, and with a little baby to look after, she needed me. But you're near grown now, Celie. I'm not needed anymore, and I've been acting like a selfish, pigheaded fool, so full of self-pity I haven't been able to see your mama's need. I've lived my life. Now it's her turn."

I couldn't believe what I was hearing. How could everything get so turned around? A few minutes ago it seemed like things were all going to work out, and now. . . ."

"Please, Gran," I said. "I don't want to go far away from here."

Gran squeezed my arm. "Celie," she said, "you're young. I know it seems hard now, but you'll meet new people, make new friends. In time the Swift River Valley will be nothin' to you but a pleasant memory."

"No, it won't," I protested. "I'll always love this place."

"You *will* always love it," Gran said. "And I'm glad of that. It means you had a good life here. But that doesn't mean you can't be happy somewhere else too."

"Then you come with us," I demanded. "I won't go if you don't come."

Gran whisked my words away with a flip of her hand. "My lands," she said, "what would I do in some newfangled place at my age? I'd be nothin' but a fish out of water. Besides, somebody's got to look after Stella—make sure she don't start goin' downhill the minute she gets to that home."

We heard a rumble and looked up. Jake was pulling up to the open doorway of the carriage house. He jumped out of his car and strode into the barn, but when he saw us he stopped in his tracks.

"Afternoon," he said, removing his hat and twisting it in his hands. "I . . . uh . . . suspect you'll want me to be moving out now?" he said to Gran.

Gran's brow furrowed.

"Don't recall saying anythin' about you moving out," she said.

"Well, I thought maybe . . . since I had to turn down your proposition . . ."

Gran didn't answer. She stood up and brushed herself off, then walked to the back of the sleigh. Jake came over and helped her down.

"Like my granddaughter said," Gran told him, "you're just doing your job. Whenever you get those papers drawn up, I'm ready to sign."

Jake's mouth fell open in surprise, and my heart sank.

21

Mama argued and argued with Gran, but she wouldn't budge an inch.

"If you don't take the money, I'll give it to the church," Gran insisted. "And I'm *goin'* to the home one way or the other, so it's your choice."

Mama knew I was upset when she came in to kiss me good night. "Don't you worry, Celie," she said. "We aren't going to let her go to any home."

But as I lay there in the darkness, I wasn't so sure. I knew what Gran was like when she got her mind made up, and I was afraid that my family was coming apart at the seams. Hours ticked by and I couldn't sleep. At last I got up, dressed quietly, and slipped down the back staircase and out through the old servants' entrance into the night.

It was clear and mild, the sky black as velvet and the stars diamond white. They hung like a twinkling canopy over the sleeping village of Enfield. I walked slowly, without fear, down the hill and along the familiar roadway into town. I knew the road so well I could walk it blindfolded. The smell of spring was heavy on the damp night air—the clean scent of new green things pushing their way up through the earth. The trees overhead were nubby with buds, and tiny peepers clung to their trunks, filling the night with a chorus of chirps. It was so peaceful—no rumble of earthmovers, no crack of the wrecker's hammer, no parade of sightseers. An owl cried. A squirrel skittered across the road. It was, just for that night, my Enfield again, and I embraced it in the aching hollows of my heart.

My feet took me, almost of their own accord, to the little apartment where Chubby and his parents lived out behind the station. I walked around to Chubby's window and tapped lightly on the pane. When he didn't respond I tapped again. Still no response. I retrieved the screwdriver we kept hidden behind the lilac bush, and I slipped the blade under the sill and pried. The old window creaked up enough for me to slip my fingers under and push it the rest of the way. I stuck my head in.

"Chubby!" I whispered.

No movement came from the lump in the bed. Chubby always had been a sound sleeper. I searched through the woods behind the house until I found a stick, then I pushed it through the window and poked Chubby in the back. He jumped.

"What the—"

"Shhsh!" I whispered.

He turned to look at me.

"Celie? What are you doing here?"

I started to speak, but before I got two words out, I was blubbering.

Chubby jumped up, threw on his pants and a sweater, then climbed out through the window. He landed with a thump on the ground beside me.

"What's wrong?" he asked, his brow furrowed with worry. "It's not that guy. . . ."

"No." I flung myself into his arms. "Oh, Chubby, it's Gran. She's selling the house and moving to a home."

"What?" Chubby pushed me back and looked at me. "What are you talking about?"

"She told me tonight. She's giving Mama the money so we can move to Chicago." I broke into sobs again.

Chubby pulled me close and let me cry for a few moments.

"Hey, c'mon," he whispered, stroking my hair gently. "She doesn't mean it. She's probably just not thinking straight."

"No." I pulled back and looked at him through the haze of my tears. "She's thinking just fine. She told me all about why she was doing it, clear as a bell. And her mind's made up, Chubby. You know how she is when her mind's made up."

Chubby stared at me a long moment, then he took my hand. "C'mon," he said. "Let's take a walk."

We walked through the dark, deserted streets of town, past the wreckage of the Swift River Hotel, by the school-house and the town hall, down to the millpond. We sat on a bench and stared at the moon's reflection in the still water. Neither of us spoke for a long time.

"Chicago . . . ," Chubby said at last. "That's so far away."

I started to cry again, and Chubby put his arm around my shoulders.

"Hey," he whispered, "we'll figure something out."

"What?" I asked.

"I don't know," he said, "but worries always seem worse at night. You know that. I'm sure things will look brighter tomorrow." He hugged me tight and kissed my forehead, and somehow I felt better.

"C'mon," he said gently. "I'll walk you home."

22

Morning dawned bright and mild, and Chubby was right. Things did seem better in the light of day. I decided that everyone was probably just overwrought yesterday after the visit to the cemetery. Something *would* work out, I was sure. It always did. And I believed Mama when she said we would never let Gran go to a home.

I pushed all those worries to the back of my mind and tried to concentrate on happier things—like the ball. It was just one day away now. When I got to school, everyone was excited. All the kids were talking about what they were planning to wear and who was supposed to be coming. Everybody in town was going to be there, and lots of people from the other valley towns too.

"The Kramer twins are even coming!" I told Chubby. "All the way from Lowell!"

"That's nice," said Chubby.

"You don't seem terribly excited," I said.

Chubby shrugged. "A dance is a dance," he said. "You still going with that drugstore cowboy?"

"Yes," I said, giggling. I had to pinch myself each time I remembered that I was actually going with Jake. Wait until the Kramer twins saw me pull up in the MG! "And it's not just a dance," I told Chubby. "It's a ball. I've got a new dress and everything!"

"Good for you," said Chubby.

"C'mon," I said. "Don't be like that. Be happy for me. I'd be happy for you if you were going with someone really special."

"Well, maybe I am," said Chubby.

"Really? Like who?"

"I guess you'll just have to wait and see," he said.

I narrowed my eyes. "You aren't going with anybody. You're just saying that."

"Like I said," said Chubby, "you'll just have to wait and see."

He walked off and I stood staring after him. "Well, if it's true I *am* happy for you," I called.

He glanced back over his shoulder.

"Thanks," he said. "I'm happy for you too."

When I got home, I took my new dress out of my wardrobe and held it up. Gran and Mama and I had all ordered dresses from the Sears catalog a few weeks back. "Never let it be said that the Wheelers didn't go out in style!" Mama had said. I had no idea where the money came from, but Gran didn't raise any objection, so I guessed she'd agreed that the ball was worth the expense.

My dress was green percale with puffed sleeves, a deep ruffled hem, and a little white organdy collar. I had loved it when I'd picked it out, but it seemed like so much had changed in the past few weeks. I didn't feel like a child anymore, and the dress looked so childish, especially when I thought about going to the ball with Jake. How I wished I could wear a grown-up gown like the one Mama had ordered. But I knew there was no chance of that. I'd just have to make myself look grown-up as best I could.

In my dressing table I still had a tube of lipstick and a small pot of rouge that Mama had given me long ago for playing dress-up, and I was planning to pin a pair of rolled up socks under my chemise so it would look like I had bosoms. Then there was the matter of stockings. . . . I still had to work on that.

"Mama," I said at supper, "I told Mr. Taylor he could have our extra ticket to the ball. I hope that's okay."

Mama considered a moment, then smiled. "Why not?" she said. "No sense in it going to waste."

"I asked him to be my escort," I added.

Gran nearly choked on her meatloaf and Mama raised her eyebrows. "Your *escort?*" she said.

"Yes." I nodded. "He doesn't really know that many people in town, and I thought it was the neighborly thing to do."

Gran frowned. "Seems to me you're gettin' mighty neighborly since that young man came along. He's near old enough to be your father, you know."

"Is not!" I protested. "He's only ten years older!" Then I blushed. "Not that it matters, of course. Like I said, I'm just being neighborly."

"What about Chubby?" asked Mama. "I just assumed you'd be going with him."

"Chubby's going with . . . somebody special," I said.

"Oh?" Mama raised her eyebrows.

"Yes," I said shortly. "We're just friends, you know."

"Um-hmm," said Mama. "Well, I suppose you can go with Mr. Taylor, but see to it that you stay in my sight all night, y'hear?"

I rolled my eyes.

"Did you *hear?*" Mama repeated.

"Yes," I answered. "I'm not deaf."

I finished my supper, then put my plate down on the floor so Ginger could lick it clean.

"By the way," I ventured on, "seeing as how I'm practically in high school now, I was thinking maybe I could wave my hair and wear silk stockings?"

"Silk stockings!" Gran blurted. "Why, I didn't wear silk stockings till my wedding day."

I rolled my eyes. "That was the olden days, Gran," I argued. "People are more modern now."

"Modern my foot," mumbled Gran. "B'sides, who do you think we are, the Rockefellers? You already got a new dress. Why, you could buy half another one for the price of a pair of silk stockings."

"You *are* a might young for silk stockings," Mama concurred.

"Oh please, Mama," I begged. "I'll surely die if I have to go to the ball in anklets. They're so babyish."

"Well then, it looks like you'll have to pick between dyin' and stayin' home," said Gran.

Mama laughed. "I'm sure you won't be the only girl your

age in anklets," she said. "Now run along and do your home-work."

I huffed out of the kitchen and sulked for the rest of the night; but as it turned out, I needn't have. Wednesday evening, as I was getting dressed, Mama came in with a package under her arm.

"It *is* quite a special occasion," she said with a smile, "and you will officially be a high school girl in a few more months. . . . "

I ripped the package open, then threw my arms around her neck. "Oh, Mama!" I cried. "You're the berries!"

Mama laughed. "They're rayon," she said, "not silk, but they're nearly as nice."

"They're perfect!" I sang. Mama gave me one of her old garter belts, and I sat right down on the bed and carefully pulled the stockings on. They felt so smooth. I held my legs straight out in front of me and turned them this way and that. "I just wish my legs weren't so hairy," I said.

"Now don't go getting any highfalutin ideas," Mama cautioned. "Nobody will ever see that peach fuzz, and you're way too young to start shaving your legs."

I stood up and looked over my shoulder.

"Are the seams straight?" I asked.

"As an arrow," said Mama.

I slipped my shoes on, then ran out and paraded in my chemise and petticoat in front of the hall mirror.

"If only I had high heels," I said.

"One more 'if only' young lady," Mama warned, "and those stockings'll go right back into my dresser drawer."

"Just teasing!" I said quickly. "They're swell. Truly." I held out my arms and twirled once more slowly in front of the mirror. With my hair loose and waved, I fancied that I looked a bit like Scarlett O'Hara. The new stockings made me feel very grown-up, at least from the waist down.

"Mama?" I sighed. "Do you think I'm ever going to get bosoms?"

Mama chuckled. "Of course you will," she said. "You're just a late bloomer. I was just like you—flat as a pancake until I was sixteen."

I sighed again. *Sixteen!* That seemed like forever. I wanted bosoms right now—tonight. I turned to examine my profile in the mirror.

"*If only* I could wear a bra," I said. Then I ran, giggling, as Mama chased me down the stairs, around the front parlor, and through the dining room. We burst into the kitchen, laughing, and then I stopped in my tracks. There, smack in the middle of the room, stood Gran—and Jake!

"Oh. I'm sorry," he said, turning red. "I just came in to borrow—"

I shrieked, crossed my arms over my chest, then turned and fled back upstairs again.

Mama flew after me.

I threw myself on the bed, my ears burning in shame. "I'm ruined!" I cried. "I'll never be able to show my face again!"

Mama sat down beside me and put a comforting hand on my back. "Oh come now," she said. "It's not like you were naked. Everything was covered. Besides, you're just a girl."

I sat up and glared at her. "No, I'm *not*!" I shouted. "But now he thinks I am. Now he knows I'm not even old enough to wear a bra!"

Mama stared at me in stony silence.

I sniffed. "What?"

"Why does it matter so much to you what Mr. Taylor thinks?" Mama asked.

I chewed my lip and my ears grew hotter.

"Celie," said Mama, "Do you have a crush on that man?"

"Of course not," I said, feeling myself blush.

"He's a grown man, Celie," Mama cautioned. "I hope you aren't mistaking his kindness for—"

"Don't you have to get dressed?" I snapped. "Tom is going to be here any minute and your hair is still up in pins."

Mama glanced at the clock. "Oh my, you're right," she said. "But—"

"I don't have a crush on anybody," I insisted.

Mama looked unconvinced, but she got up anyway. "All right," she said. "Finish getting dressed, and we'll all ride over together in Tom's car. Gran, too."

"*Tom's* car? But I told all my friends. . . ."

Mama looked at me pointedly. "Told all your friends what?" she asked.

"Nothing," I grumbled.

23

Jake and Tom were waiting in the parlor with Gran by the time I got downstairs again. I didn't know how I was going to meet Jake's eyes, but he made it easy.

"Ah," he said. "You *are* wearing clothes! What a relief. I thought we were going to be the talk of the town."

I giggled. "Sorry," I said. "I didn't know you were here."

"My fault," he said gallantly. "I should have made more noise." He looked so handsome in his double-breasted gray suit, just like he'd stepped out of a Chicago Woolen Mills catalog. Tom looked like a country bumpkin by comparison, his old brown suit so ill-fitting that I wondered if he'd borrowed it from a smaller man.

"May I say, Miss Wheeler," Jake said with a courtly dip of his head, "that you are looking quite elegant this evening. I daresay you take after your grandmother." He turned and smiled at Gran, who did look lovely. Her snow-white hair was all primped and curled, and her new pink and gray voile dress flattered her fragile figure. She pursed her lips at Jake's compliment and mumbled under her breath.

"You do look real pretty, Gran," I allowed.

Gran smiled at me. "So do you, dear," she said, then she squinted her eyes and peered at me more closely. "Is there something on your face, Cecelia?" she asked.

I groaned inwardly. "What?" I said, stepping back into the shadows so my rouge and lipstick would not be so obvious.

"Looks to me like—"

"Oh, I nearly forgot," Jake suddenly interrupted. He walked over to where he'd left his white fedora lying on a table and produced a couple of small white tissue packets from beneath it. "For the two loveliest ladies in Enfield," he said, handing one to Gran, then turning and handing the other to me. With his back to Gran, he gave me a conspiratorial wink. I smiled at him gratefully.

The packets contained lovely little corsages of baby roses—red for Gran, yellow for me.

"Oh, they're beautiful!" I said.

"May I?" asked Jake, offering to pin mine on.

"Oh, yes, please."

He leaned close and I could smell his Old Spice cologne. His hair brushed my cheek, and I nearly swooned. "How's that?" he asked.

"Perfect," I said, gazing raptly into his eyes.

"May I help you with yours?" Jake asked, turning toward Gran. But Gran already had hers on.

"No need," she said shortly, but then her voice softened and she added, "thank you."

"Thank *you*," Jake replied, "for allowing me to accompany you and your family on this special occasion."

The way Jake said "special" reminded me suddenly of what the ball was all about. It was easy to forget in all the commotion, but at midnight, Enfield, my hometown, would cease to exist. Gran was quiet, too, and I knew all thoughts of me and my lipstick were lost in her contemplation of the night's events.

There were footsteps on the stairs and we all turned just as Mama entered the room.

Jake gave out a loud wolf whistle, which caused Gran to stiffen and throw him a stern glance.

"I'm sorry," he apologized, first to Gran then to Mama, then to Tom. "I'm just not used to so much beauty in one room. I'm afraid I forgot my manners."

Mama blushed prettily, and I couldn't help but feel a twinge of jealousy. She looked *so* elegant. Her gown of peacock blue chiffon highlighted her eyes and clung softly to the curves of her tall, slender figure. Her hair hugged her head Jean Harlow-style in a little cap of golden finger waves, and on her feet were delicate ankle-strap pumps dyed to match her dress. I felt frumpy and frilly by comparison.

Tom stepped forward awkwardly and handed Mama a corsage. "You sure *do* look beautiful, Miss Helen," he said.

"Why thank you, Tom." Mama blushed again. "Would you pin it on for me, please?"

Tom turned red as a ripe summer raspberry. I cringed as he fumbled with Mama's corsage, certain he was going to jab her at any moment.

"I'm sorry, Miss Helen," he apologized in frustration. "I'm just all thumbs when it comes to things like this."

I was about to take over the task when Jake suddenly stepped forward.

"May I?" he asked Tom.

"Well . . . sure, I guess," said Tom. He reluctantly handed over the corsage.

Jake leaned over Mama before she had a chance to object and adeptly pinned the flowers in place.

"Seems you had a lot of experience at such things, Mr. Taylor," Mama teased.

Jake dipped his head, as if tipping his hat, and gave Mama a beguiling smile. "Some," he admitted.

"Shouldn't we be going?" I announced loudly.

"Indeed," said Mama, taking Tom's arm. "We'll be lucky as it is to find a parking space."

Jake turned to Gran. "After you, madam," he said with a courtly bow.

Gran sniffed and walked past, mumbling something under her breath about putting on airs.

Jake winked at me and offered his arm. I slipped my arm through his and floated out to the car on a cloud.

By the time we arrived downtown there was a huge traffic jam. Hundreds of people were thronging toward the town hall, more people than I had ever seen downtown before, more people, I thought, than our little town hall could possibly hold. Firemen were directing traffic.

"There's Herb Colebrook," said Gran, pointing to the former police chief. "Pull up and let me have a word with him, please."

Tom slowed the Model T in front of the town hall and Gran stuck her head out of the car window.

"Elizabeth!" said Mr. Colebrook when he saw her. "Been saving a spot for you." Everyone in town knew and respected Gran. She had served the town in many capacities over the years—on the town council, the school board, as president of the Quabbin Club, chairwoman of many charitable organizations. Herb motioned to Tom. "Pull down around behind the town hall," he said. "We've set that lot aside for our upstanding local citizens."

"Thank you kindly, Herb," Gran said as we pulled away.

"Hurry up if you want to get inside," Herb hollered after us. "We're going to have to close her up pretty soon."

Sure enough, not long after we squeezed inside the big double doors of the town hall, word went out that the building was filled beyond capacity and no more tickets would be sold. Almost a thousand people were crowded inside, but nearly two thousand more had to be turned away.

"Where on earth could all these people be coming from?" I asked Mama.

"From all the towns around," she said. "And lots of them are folks that moved away years ago but still feel a tie to the valley."

"Plus the project workers," Jake added. "I recognize a lot of the engineers and crewmen here."

"And reporters," Gran put in. "The place is swarming with 'em, hoping to catch pictures of us all crying I s'pose."

For a moment a shadow dimmed my excitement. At twelve midnight, this building would be a town hall without a town. An eerie little shiver ran up my spine.

"Celie! Celie, over here!" Two arms were flailing above the crowd and when I stood on tiptoes I saw it was the Kramer twins working their way toward me. When they broke through the crowd we all hugged one another and admired one another's dresses, then I walked back over and took Jake's arm.

"Jake," I said, "may I present my dear friends Mary and Kate Kramer."

The twins stared at Jake dumbfounded.

Jake took Mary's right hand and then Kate's and touched them each in turn to his lips. "Charmed," he said. The girls looked about ready to swoon.

"Likewise, I'm sure," they mumbled.

"Did you come with dates?" I asked them.

"Oh, no," said Mary, recovering her voice. "We thought we'd just spend the evening with all of our old friends."

"Well, here come some of them now," I said, nodding at a clump of classmates who were fighting their way toward us through the crowd.

From inside the great hall we heard the orchestra tuning up.

"We'd better be going in," I said to Jake. "See you inside," I told the girls as we walked away, leaving them still staring after us openmouthed.

The great hall was set up like an auditorium, with a stage and hundreds of folding chairs. More chairs were arranged upstairs in the gallery. It looked beautiful, all draped in red, white, and blue, with flowers everywhere. We were all dressed in our best. Some of the men, whom I'd never before seen in anything but overalls, looked as awkward as trussed-up turkeys in their stiff-collared suits and ties. Many of the women had pretty new dresses, like Mama, but others had made do with older things. Some, like Trudy Ward Stafford, wore their wedding gowns. Even old Mrs. McGill, who was usually mean as two pins and cross as a whole paper of 'em, looked genteel in her pink dimity dress. The children were all gussied up too—little girls in ruffles and patent leathers, little boys in bow ties and knee pants. I caught a glimpse of Chubby up near the stage.

"Chubby," I called. He turned and I waved, and then I saw who was on his arm.

Belinda!

I could feel my jaw tighten as the two of them made their way back toward Jake and me. Chubby had invited her just to irritate me, I was sure.

Belinda looked ravishing. Her long, golden hair shimmered with light, and she wore a sleek floor-length silken gown that looked *so* much more grown-up than mine. I felt frumpier than ever.

"Good evening," said Chubby with a courtly dip of his head. He was wearing a jacket and tie, and he had his hair stylishly slicked back with pomade. I was surprised at how grown-up he looked.

"Jake," I said through clenched teeth, "may I present my *friend* Chubby Miller and . . . his *date*, Belinda Wilder."

"My pleasure," said Jake. He nodded to Chubby, then bowed to Belinda.

"Likewise, I'm sure," said Belinda, batting her eyelashes at Jake.

I gave her a sugary sweet smile and clung all the more tightly to Jake's arm.

24

The town hall was soon stifling hot. It had been another unseasonably warm day—near ninety degrees—and with the size of the crowd, the hall heated up like an oven.

"Jeepers," I said as I sat fanning myself with my program book. "If they don't get started soon, I'm going to melt right down into a big green puddle."

Jake laughed. "I'm sure they got held up because of the crowd," he said. He took out a handkerchief and wiped his brow. "I'm with you, though. I don't know how much more of this heat I can stand."

Finally, at just about eight o'clock, McEnelly's Orchestra started to play. They played mostly old favorites, like "Put on Your Old Gray Bonnet," "Bicycle Built for Two," and "Dream a Little Dream." In between songs people made speeches—Doc Seaver, Mr. Howell, Mr. Hill, one of the engineers. They spoke about the past, about how much we had shared as a community. They reminisced about the good times, like the taffy pulls and quilting bees, the Fourth of July picnics and church socials, the annual Sugaring Off each March, and the strawberry festival each June. And then they talked about the bad times too—the mill closings, the fires, the young men going off to war. Through it all, the good and bad, they reminded us how much the valley had given us, how much we had learned from one another. By the time the orchestra ended the program with "Till we Meet Again," we were all blubbering like it was a funeral.

It was a relief when the band finally struck up the grand march. Doc and Mrs. Seaver led the first round. Then Mr. Hill and Mrs. Briggs led another round, and finally it was time to clear the chairs away for dancing.

Both Jake and Tom seemed a bit sheepish. I suppose they felt somewhat guilty because of their connection to the project.

"Can we get you ladies something?" Jake asked. "Some punch, maybe?"

"That would be nice, thank you," said Mama, and Jake and Tom headed for the refreshment stand.

I slumped against the wall.

"I feel like a dishrag," I said, "inside and out."

Mama nodded. "I feel a bit wrung out myself," she said. Gran said nothing, but she looked tired and drawn.

By the time Tom and Jake got back with the punch, the dance music had begun. I didn't feel much like dancing at first, but then I saw Chubby and Belinda out on the floor and suddenly I changed my mind.

"You want to dance?" I asked Jake.

"That's what I came for," he said with a charming grin. He offered me his arm and led me out on the floor. Mama and Tom followed us and, two by two, other couples joined in. Even Gran came out on the arm of old Mr. Wallace.

The band was playing "The Way You Look Tonight." Jake slid his arm around my waist and looked into my eyes, and suddenly everything else flew out of my mind. There I was, actually in Jake's arms! My heart started thumping and my head got light. We started to move, but my feet felt like bricks. I had had dancing lessons in school, of course, but I'd always been better at climbing trees than fox-trotting. I stumbled over Jake's shoes and stepped on his toes.

"I'm sorry." I mumbled. "I'm not very good at this."

Jake smiled kindly into my eyes. "Just relax," he said. "Let me lead you. Can you feel the pressure of my hand on your back?"

I nodded.

"Good. Now just listen to the music and move the way I'm guiding you. It might help if you closed your eyes."

I grinned. "Okay," I said. "I'll try."

Jake's arms were strong and his hand firm on my back. I closed my eyes and let the music flow through me, allowing myself to relax and follow the push and pull of Jake's hand. Soon, to my amazement, we were moving smoothly together.

Jake rested his cheek against my hair. "You're l-o-v-e-ly," he sang softly along with the orchestra, repeating in my ear the words that the singer was crooning. I didn't dare allow myself to believe that Jake meant the words he was singing, but still . . . it was so romantic.

I sighed dreamily. Please God, I thought, don't let this song ever end. Then, *thump!* Who should we bump into but Chubby and Belinda! I couldn't help noticing how handsome Chubby looked. He wasn't pretty-boy handsome, like

Jake, but there was undoubtedly a rugged, outdoorsy charm about him. He and Belinda made an infuriatingly attractive couple.

I caught his eye and gave him a "Why are you with *her?*" scowl.

He gave me a "Why are you with *him?*" scowl right back, and we both turned away from each another in disgust.

"Something wrong?" asked Jake.

"No," I said. "It's just that this song is sort of . . . slow."

As if he'd heard me, the orchestra leader suddenly picked up the tempo and launched into Glenn Miller's "In the Mood."

"Lindy hop?" asked Jake.

"And how!" I shouted. Now we were in my territory. I'd listened to the *Hit Parade* almost every Saturday night for years. When the twins used to live up the street, they often came over, and we'd all lindy hop around the parlor. Sometimes Chubby would come, too, but dancing wasn't ever one of his favorite pastimes. You'd never know it to look at him now, though. He and Belinda were jumpin' and jivin' up a storm. I was beginning to suspect that Chubby was trying to make me jealous. Well, I'd show him.

Jake grabbed my hand and gave me a twirl, and I started putting on a performance worthy of Ginger Rogers. It was obvious that Jake was no slouch when it came to swing, either. "In the Mood" was one kicking-out tune, but he was keeping right up with me. Before long a lot of couples began to tire and leave the floor—eventually even Chubby and Belinda. I was determined to stick it out till the end, though, and when the clarinet climbed up the scale and screamed out the last note, Jake grabbed me around the waist and hoisted me high over his head. Everyone burst out clapping, then Jake lowered me down and we fell into each other's arms, laughing.

"Having fun now?" asked Jake.

I smiled. "And how!"

Out of the corner of my eye I saw Chubby scowling.

The next number was a good old-fashioned square dance, and somehow Chubby ended up as my corner, and Belinda ended up as Jake's. I decided to ignore them both and focus all my attention on Jake. This time it was his turn to be the clumsy one. "Sorry," he said as we bumped heads doing "Duck for the Apple." "We don't do much square-dancing in Boston."

"You'll get the hang of it," I said.

When it came time to swing with my corner, Chubby grabbed my arm. "You're making a fool of yourself, you know," he whispered. "That guy is just using you."

"Don't be ridiculous," I snapped back. "Using me for what?"

"I don't know," said Chubby as we promenaded. "I haven't figured out his angle yet."

"That's because he doesn't have one," I snapped. "And talk about angles, what's Belinda's?"

"What do you mean?" asked Chubby.

I laughed. "You don't think she really wants to be with you, do you? She's using you to get close to me."

"Close to you? Why?"

"That's why." I nodded across the floor where Belinda was promenading with Jake, making goo-goo eyes at him all the while.

"He doesn't seem to be minding it," said Chubby.

Jake *did* seem to be enjoying Belinda's attention.

"I hate these stupid square dances," I huffed.

Chubby laughed.

"Promenade that lady home," shouted the caller. "Now swing with your partner."

I grabbed Jake's arm away from Belinda, glad that the dance was nearly at an end.

"Phew!" said Jake when it was over. "I don't know about you, but I could use some air."

"Me too," I said, wiping my brow with the back of my hand. "It's sizzling in here. Come on. It'll be less crowded out back." As the band struck up another tune, I grabbed Jake's hand and pulled him quickly through the crowd before Belinda could follow. We pushed the back door open and stepped out onto a small porch. The temperature had dropped considerably, and the night air was wonderfully cool and refreshing.

Jake leaned on the railing and looked up at the sky. It was clear and bright with stars. Below us, beyond the parking lot, the millpond rippled softly in the moonlight. "Sure is peaceful around here," said Jake.

"Have you ever lived in the country?" I asked.

"Nope. Boston city born and bred. A fella could get used to living like this, though."

"Are you . . . thinking about maybe settling down around these parts?" I asked.

"Hey, Jake!" someone yelled before Jake could answer.

We looked down and saw a young couple leaning against the hood of a car. The man was waving.

"Mike," Jake called back. "Didn't know you were here."

Jake turned to me. "Friend of mine from the job," he said. "Come on down. I'll introduce you."

The two of us walked down the stairs and the couple came over to meet us. "Jake," said the man called Mike, "this is my girl, Eva."

Jake dipped his head to Eva. "Pleasure," he said. Then he turned to me. "This is Cecelia," he said, and I held my breath, wondering what he would say next. "Guess you could say she's my girl too," he said with a wink. "At least for tonight."

Mike and Eva laughed and I felt humiliated. They didn't take Jake seriously for a moment. It was obvious they considered me a child.

Mike pulled out a pack of Lucky Strikes. He offered one to Eva, who accepted, then passed right over me and offered one to Jake, who declined. Mike struck a match and Eva leaned forward, elegantly holding her cigarette in front of her lips. She sucked in until the flame caught, then she took a long, dramatic puff. How I yearned to look that elegant, that grown-up. Mike lit his own cigarette, then moved to put the pack back in his pocket.

"I'd like one," I heard myself saying.

Mike paused. "What?" he asked.

"A cigarette," I said. "I'd like one, if you don't mind."

Jake looked at me doubtfully. "You sure that would be okay with your folks?"

I bristled. "Of course," I said shortly, taking a quick glance around to be sure neither Mama nor Gran were in sight. "I smoke all the time."

Mike shrugged. "Okay," he said, tapping another cigarette

out of the pack. "But you'd better be careful. These things'll stunt your growth."

I laughed awkwardly, then bent and accepted the light he offered. I straightened and took a long, dramatic puff the way I'd seen Eva do it. The smoke felt like a saw blade slicing across the back of my throat. I tried not to cough, but I couldn't help myself.

Jake grinned. "Tastes good, huh?" he said wryly.

"And how," I lied, my face coloring up as I took another, smaller puff.

There was a group of men standing around and laughing down at the other end of the parking lot. "That's Bill and the boys," Mike said to Jake. "Want to go say hello?"

"Sure," said Jake, then he turned to me. "Will you excuse me for a moment?"

"Of course," I said, waving him off with my cigarette.

Jake and Mike sauntered down to join the group. I smiled knowingly as I saw the others clap them on the back and pass around something small and dark. I'd known for years that whenever men gathered outside a function for a "breath of air," there was usually a flask being passed.

The back door of the town hall creaked open, and I looked up to see who was there. The door opened wider and Chubby stepped out. I frowned and hid my cigarette behind my back.

"Hey. What are you doing down there?" he called.

"Nothing."

He tripped down the stairs. "What's that behind your back?" he asked.

I glared at him. "Excuse me," I said to Eva as I steered him off to one side.

"I smell cigarette smoke," he said.

I brought the cigarette out again and boldly took a puff. "So what?" I challenged him.

"So—you know your grandmother doesn't hold with smoking."

"I don't see what business that is of yours," I snapped. "Besides, everybody smokes these days. Gran's just old-fashioned."

"Not *everybody* smokes," said Chubby. "I don't. I think it stinks."

"Well," I said, taking another puff and blowing it in his face, "maybe you're just not grown-up enough yet to appreciate the finer things."

Chubby frowned. "Go cook a radish," he said as he pushed past me and stalked off into the night.

A nervous tension began to build in the ballroom as the clock ticked on toward midnight. All the dancing and noise couldn't hide it. I looked for Gran and saw that she was still on the arm of old Mr. Wallace, a good place for her. The Wallace family had lived in Enfield for generations, nearly as long as Gran's. They considered one another kin. Mama was sitting on a chair along the wall, looking bored. Tom, who sat droopy-eyed beside her, looked like he'd gone out for one too many "breaths of air."

Just shortly before midnight, Doc Seaver signaled the band to stop playing, and a hush fell over the crowd. Jake and I stood still, watching and waiting as the clock ticked off the final minutes. *Dong, Dong* . . . it began chiming midnight.

Muffled sounds of sobbing broke out all around the room, and instantly my eyes filled with tears too. I brushed them away awkwardly. I looked over at Gran. She was dabbing at her eyes with a handkerchief. Mr. Wallace took out his handkerchief, blew his nose, and quickly wiped his eyes too. Old friends embraced. Husbands tried to hold back their own tears while comforting their wives. Even little kids sniffled and sobbed. I looked around for Chubby and Belinda, but I couldn't see them in the crowd.

The band started softly playing "Auld Lang Syne" and people began to dance again, holding tightly to one another, many of them still crying.

"You want to dance again?" Jake asked quietly.

"No," I said. "Will you excuse me a moment?"

Suddenly, all I wanted was to find Chubby.

25

Chubby wasn't anywhere in the hall. I found Belinda making time with some young sailor I'd never seen before.

"Where's Chubby?" I asked her.

"Who?" she asked.

"Chubby," I repeated, "your *date*."

"Oh . . ." Belinda twittered and batted her eyes at the sailor. "You don't think I came with Chubby, do you? We just had a dance or two—for old times' sake, that's all."

I frowned. "I see," I said. "Where is he?"

"I don't know," said Belinda. "I haven't seen him in over an hour."

The twins hadn't seen him, either, or any of the boys. His mother thought maybe he'd gotten tired or bored and gone on home. I didn't think so. It wasn't like Chubby to miss out on an event as important as the end of Enfield.

The end of Enfield. I shivered. It was over. Our town was

gone, at least on paper, and soon it would be gone completely, wiped off the map as though it had never existed. And what did that make all of us, the people in this room? People from nowhere? I watched my friends and neighbors out on the dance floor. They looked like people from nowhere—moving their feet, going on, while their eyes held a lost look, a frightened look, like little chicks hopping after their mother, crying, "Don't leave me. Don't leave me."

Chubby, where are you? I hurried toward the back door where I'd seen him last. It was quiet out on the landing. The cluster of men by the parking lot had broken up and gone back inside. I walked down the steps, away from the building and the muffled sounds of the orchestra.

"Chubby?" I called tentatively into the darkness. There was no answer. I walked down as far as the schoolhouse. Then, from down the other end of the millpond, I heard a splash and a voice singing, "Five foot two, eyes of blue, Coochie, coochie, coochie, coo, Has anybody seen my girl?"

I walked along the bank until I saw Chubby sitting cross-legged at the edge of the pond, aimlessly skipping stones across the water.

I approached him quietly.

"Chubby?" I said.

He looked up, startled for a moment, then he frowned. "Whadd'you want?" he asked. His voice sounded oddly thick.

"Are you all right?" I asked.

"Whadd'you care?" he slurred.

"Have you been drinking?" I asked.

"None of your bizniz," said Chubby.

"Chubby Miller," I said, "you *have* been drinking! Are you screwy? Your folks'll skin you alive!"

"I don' care," he said sullenly.

"You don't care? What is *wrong* with you?"

Chubby winged another stone across the pond. "Nothin'," he said bitterly.

I sighed. "Mind if I sit down?" I asked.

Chubby looked up at me again, then beyond me, back toward the town hall.

"Where's your *date?*" he asked.

"Same place yours is," I said. "Back there, probably dancing with somebody else."

Chubby shrugged. "Ah, who cares anyway?"

I sat down beside him. "You're missing the ball," I told him. "You missed midnight."

Chubby stared back at me sullenly. "So?" he grumbled.

"Chubby," I said, "what's going on? It's not like you to act like this."

Chubby slammed a rock into the water, then he looked at me defiantly.

"You and I have been best friends since the first grade," he said. "It was supposed to be you and me tonight, Celie. Not *him*. What does he care about Enfield? What does he care about us? It was supposed to be you and me together when the clock struck twelve."

I swallowed hard. "I know," I said quietly. "That's why I came looking for you."

Chubby looked at me skeptically. "Really?"

"Yes, really," I said. "I wanted to have the last dance with you, and now look at you. You can't even dance."

"Sh—sure I can," said Chubby. He pushed himself up to his feet and stumbled sideways a step.

"*Sure* you can," I said, getting to my feet too. "C'mon, they're serving sandwiches and coffee at the grange. Let's get some food into you."

I put my arm around Chubby's waist. He swayed a little. "I lub you, Celie," he said.

I smiled. "I know. I love you too. Now come on."

"No," said Chubby. "I really, *really* lub you."

"And I really, really love you too," I said. "Now come on—one foot in front of the other."

After a couple of sandwiches and as many cups of coffee, Chubby sobered up enough to go back to the dance. When we got to the hall, Tom was slumped down in his chair, asleep against the wall, Belinda was dancing with her sailor, and Mama and Jake were doing the Charleston to "Yes Sir, That's My Baby." Chubby and I joined in.

"Where've you two been?" Mama asked. "We were about to come looking."

"Just went out to get some air," I said. "Where's Gran?"

"She got tired, and Mr. Wallace did us the favor of taking her home."

Jake and Mama and Chubby and I all took turns dancing with one another until the orchestra leader announced the last dance. Both Jake and Chubby looked at me. I had come with Jake and it was customary that we should dance the last dance, but I had promised this dance to Chubby.

"Chubby and I were always dancing partners in school," I started to explain, "and tonight being the last night. . . ."

"Say no more," said Jake gallantly. "My heart is broken, but I will bear it bravely." He turned to Mama. "Good lady," he said, "will you do me the honor of taking your daughter's place lest the others in the company look upon me with pity?" He bowed low to Mama, and we all laughed.

The orchestra struck up the final song, and Chubby slipped his arm around my waist. I put my hand on his shoulder and we started to move, then he pulled me closer and leaned his chin against my hair. His shoulders were broad, almost as broad as Jake's, and he smelled of bay rum cologne. I felt so at home with his arms around me, his heart beating close to mine. I remembered his slurred profession of affection down by the pond and a surge of tenderness washed over me. Then the memory of our almost-kiss at Greenwich Lake flashed through my mind, and for a moment I found myself tempted to turn my face to his. But that was crazy. This was Chubby. I took a deep breath. It was just the night, I told myself. Just the sentimentality of the night, and the last dance.

The song was "Home Sweet Home." "Mid pleasures and palaces though may we roam," sang the orchestra singer, "be it ever so humble, there's no place like home." I looked around me at the friends and neighbors I had grown up with—the Doubledays, Webbers, Howells, Seavers—and a deep sorrow settled over me, a sorrow I saw mirrored in all their faces. "To thee I'll return, overburdened with care; The heart's dearest solace will smile on me there; No more from that cottage again will I roam; Be it ever so humble, there's no place like home."

The last strains of music faded away, and Chubby and I parted but didn't leave the floor. No one did. We all just stood there looking around at one another awkwardly, no one knowing what to say, no one wanting to be the first to leave. At last, Lewis Janes, the janitor, flicked the lights. "It's all over, folks," he said gently. "Time to lock up."

Sniffling and dabbing at their eyes with handkerchiefs, folks began slowly moving toward the exits.

"Come on," said Mama. "Time to go."

She and Jake woke Tom, then headed for the doors. Chubby and I took a last look around, then Chubby took my hand and we walked out together. Still, no one was in a hurry to depart. We lingered outside for some time longer, saying good-bye again to friends who had come back for the evening and listening to others discuss what their plans were, now that the end was in sight.

"What about you?" folks asked Mama. "Have you and your mother-in-law decided what you're going to do?"

"We're still discussing it," Mama said, "just taking things one day at a time."

"Well, that's all any of us can do isn't it?" said one of the neighbors.

A reporter milled about in the crowd, asking people for their thoughts on the town's demise. "The young people can stand it," I heard seventy-seven-year-old Benjamin Rowan say. "Us old fellows are going to find it tough. We don't make new acquaintances. We've got to move away, and outside of our own kin, we'll be forced to live the rest of our lives among strangers. Every old person feels it on that account."

26

Jake brought the sale papers home the next night. Gran read them through from end to end, sitting at the kitchen table, then she signed with a shaky hand. I watched her with a heavy heart. *Someday* was breathing down my neck.

"Thank you, Mrs. Wheeler," said Jake. "I hope you think you got a fair deal."

Gran nodded abruptly, then got to her feet. "I'm goin' out for a walk," she said.

"I'll go with you, Gran," I offered, but she shook her head.

"Nope," she said. "I'm goin' alone."

We watched out of the kitchen window as she walked past the carriage house and out into the fields. Her step was slow and her back bowed.

"Poor thing," whispered Mama. Tears swam in her eyes.

"Maybe I should go after her," I said.

"No." Mama shook her head. "She needs some time alone. She'll be all right."

I sank down into my chair, rested my elbows on the table, and rested my chin in my hands.

"I hate Boston," I said glumly.

"Hey," said Jake, "I can't take all these sad faces. I've got an idea that might cheer everybody up."

"What's that?" asked Mama.

"Wait here." Jake ran out to his car and came back with a long, narrow box under his arm. He put it down on the kitchen table.

I brightened. "Monopoly!" I said. "That *is* keen. Orville Tate has it and it's the berries."

"I've never heard of it," said Mama.

"You pretend you're a rich tycoon," I told her, "and you buy and sell land and houses and hotels. . . ."

Mama flinched. "That's hitting a little close to home just now, don't you think?" she said.

I sighed. "I suppose so. It is fun, though. And it's just a game."

Mama smiled and nodded. "You're right," she said. "We could do with a little diversion. Let's give it a try."

Jake pulled out a chair and sat down, and Mama put some glasses and a pitcher of lemonade on the table. "I was hoping your grandmother might join in," said Jake. "I thought it might take her mind off the sale."

"I wouldn't count on it," I told him. "I think Monopoly is a little too modern for Gran's taste."

"And like I said," Mama put in, "I don't think Gran would find buyin' and sellin' property very entertaining just now."

"I suppose you're right," said Jake. "I'm sorry. I should have thought about that."

"No offense taken," said Mama. "It's just a game, as Celie says, and I'm sure we'll have fun with it."

And we did have fun. We wheeled and dealed and laughed, and before long Mama and Jake were on a first-name basis. It felt good to get lost in the game and forget about the real world, about the fact that our own house had just been bought out from under us. Mama seemed to be having the most fun of all. "My lands," she cried, when Jake landed on her Park Place hotel and had to pay her ten thousand dollars. "Can you imagine if this money was real?"

"What's all this racket?" asked Gran, coming into the house with a disapproving frown. "I can hear you clear out to the apple orchard. Is this some kind of a celebration?"

"No, Gran. It's a game," I explained. "Jake brought it in to help take our minds off things. Come join us. It's keen."

Gran shook her head and walked on by. "Time for the *Headlines News*," she mumbled.

May came in a few days later, balmy and sweet. It wasn't like other years, though, with the world turning new and green outside the schoolroom window, giving us all a hopeless case of spring fever. Instead, the town turned bleaker and browner, with machinery drowning out the birdsongs, and dust clouds sweeping through the streets. More and more buildings were pounded to rubble, and more and more trees were chopped down and hauled away. For a while we remained above the devastation at home on the mountain, but bit by bit it began creeping toward us.

Gran grew quieter and more distant. She seemed lost in

her own world much of the time, and if you spoke to her, it took a while for her eyes to focus, and even then it didn't seem like the words were getting through. She still wouldn't talk about moving, still insisted she was going to a home.

Mama had become strangely quiet on the subject, too, though she still spent every spare minute in her room, practicing on the old treadle sewing machine. Things didn't look promising, but I still kept hoping against hope that somehow she'd change her mind about Chicago.

Jake worked hard at trying to cheer us all up, and I was growing fonder of him with each passing day. I'd help him wash his car on Saturdays, and sometimes we'd go out for a ride or another driving lesson. Evenings he'd bring Monopoly down, or we'd play cards or have checker tournaments out on the porch. Sometimes, when he wasn't looking, I would just watch him, thinking how handsome he was, how wonderful in every way. I dreamed of being his girl, maybe even his wife someday. But there were two problems with our relationship—Mama and Chubby.

Mama seemed determined not to leave Jake and me alone for a moment, so she kept horning in on everything we did. She acted silly around Jake, too, laughing too loud and making goofy jokes. It was embarrassing. Jake didn't seem to mind, though. After a while, he just started automatically including her in all our plans, which irritated me to no end.

Chubby, on the other hand, continued to have no use whatsoever for Jake and seemed to resent it whenever Jake was around. That put me in the hard position of having to constantly choose between the two men I cared most about in the world. I wanted to spend as much time as possible with

Chubby, especially since our remaining days together might be numbered, but my heart yearned to be with Jake too. Then Jake and Mama started palling around together when I wasn't home, and it got so that I hated to go anywhere for fear that they might start enjoying themselves too much without me.

One Saturday I came home early from a birthday party for just that reason, and sure enough they were nowhere to be found.

"Where are Mama and Jake?" I asked Gran.

"Went for a walk," said Gran.

"Where?"

"Up through the orchard, I think," said Gran.

I started for the door.

"Celie," said Gran, "why don't you just let your mama and Jake be for a while?"

I turned around. "Why?"

"They're just enjoyin' each other's company," said Gran.

I frowned. "There's something I've got to tell Mama," I lied, then I dashed out of the door before Gran could stop me.

I bolted across the driveway toward the orchard and was starting up the hill when I heard Mama's laugh. I turned to see the barn door slide open. Out walked Mama and Jake.

"Hey!" I shouted.

Mama's head spun.

"Celie?" she said. "When did you get home?"

"Just now," I said. I stomped over to where they were standing.

"What were you doing in the barn?" I asked.

Mama blushed and glanced at Jake. "Just . . . showing Jake around," she said.

"With the door shut?" I demanded.

Mama frowned. "Celie, that's really not your—"

"Say," Jake interrupted, "I don't know about you two, but I'm a bit dry. What do you say we all take a ride over to Warton for a soda?"

"I'm not thirsty," I snapped, glaring at Mama.

Mama stared back at me in silence for a moment, then she glanced at Jake.

"Thank you for the offer, Jake," she said, "but I've got some things I need to tend to before supper."

Jake nodded. "All right then," he said. "I'll just go on up to my room and do some paperwork."

Jake walked away and I followed Mama into the house.

"You're making a fool of yourself, you know," I hissed, "throwing yourself at Jake. You're way too old for him."

"And you're way too young," Mama said pointedly. "I thought you said you and Jake were just friends, Celie."

I fumed internally, but I knew I had to be careful not to show my true feelings. "We are," I said offhandedly. "But we're a lot younger than you, and we get tired of having an old person always barging in on everything we do."

Mama chuckled. "Jake doesn't seem to mind my company," she said.

"He's just too polite to say anything," I told her.

Mama didn't reply—just gave me a smug, patronizing smile, which irritated me all the more.

Gran, who was reading the paper at the kitchen table, clicked her tongue. "Sounds to me like that man is turnin' both your heads," she said.

"Is *not*," I shouted, then I huffed up to my room.

•   •   •

Not long after that Chubby came over and joined us for Monopoly one evening. He was edgy and out of sorts and was so rude to Jake that I finally had to walk him outside and talk to him privately.

"Look, Chubby," I said, "just because we're best friends doesn't mean you can run my life. If you can't be nice to Jake you'd just better stop coming around."

"You're not still carrying a torch for that guy, are you?" Chubby snapped.

I blushed. "That's none of your business," I said.

"Well, you're wasting your time if you are," Chubby groused. "It's your ma he's got his eye on. Can't you see that?"

I bristled. "Don't be ridiculous, Chubby Miller," I said. "Mama's way too old for Jake."

"And you're way too young."

"I think that's up to Jake to decide," I said.

From back in the kitchen came a peal of Jake's deep laughter followed by Mama's giddy twittering.

"Yes," said Chubby wryly, "I guess it is."

There were footsteps and then Mama pushed the screen door open. Jake followed behind her.

"Oh, hi," she said, a bit awkwardly. "It's such a lovely evening. Jake and I thought we'd take a walk." She and Jake stepped off the porch and started strolling toward the road.

Chubby gave me a knowing smile.

"Wait a minute," I called after her. "I'll come with you."

Mama looked back at me and hesitated. "What about Chubby?" she asked.

"Chubby was just leaving," I said pointedly.

Chubby scowled at me. "Yeah," he said, shoving his hands in his pockets. "I got places to go and things to do."

I hurried to catch up with Mama and Jake and pushed my way in between them.

"So, where are we going?" I asked.

"Celie," said Mama, "Jake and I were planning to walk in to town for a beer. It'll be past your bedtime by the time we get back."

My bedtime! I was indignant. "I'm not a child, Mother!"

"Just the same," said Mama, "I think you've been neglecting your studies lately. I think it would be well for you to do a little homework, then get to bed."

I looked from her to Jake and back again, Chubby's words still jabbing at me like a pitchfork. *It's your ma he's got his eye on.*

"I am not neglecting my studies," I blurted. "You're just trying to get rid of me."

"Celie," said Mama, "you're talking silly now."

"I am not," I shouted at her. "You're trying to get rid of me because you want Jake for yourself!"

Mama turned beet red. "Celie!" she said. "Mind your tongue."

"I will not," I said. "It's the truth. That's why you're always hanging around us, mooning after him like a lovesick cow."

Mama looked stricken. She turned to Jake and put a hand to her head.

"I'm . . . I'm sorry," she stammered. "I don't know where she gets these ideas. She's obviously distraught. . . ."

Jake slid a comforting arm around Mama's shoulders. "It's okay," he said. "I've been thinking for a while that maybe Celie and I need to have a talk." He looked at me. "Celie," he said, "I'm sorry if you've mistaken my attention for something it isn't. I was just trying to be friendly, just trying to fill up some of the space your father and Cal left in your life."

I swallowed hard, and my face flushed hot as a poker. How could I have been so wrong? Here I'd been thinking of Jake as Rhett Butler all this time, and he'd been thinking of me as Little Orphan Annie. I looked down at the ground.

"So Chubby was right, then?" I said quietly.

"Right?" asked Jake. "About what?"

I looked up again. "About you and Mama," I said. "Chubby said it was Mama you fancied all along."

Mama's color deepened again, and she dropped her eyes.

Jake cleared his throat and dropped his arm from Mama's shoulders.

"Your mama's a fine lady," he sputtered, "and I've enjoyed her company, that's true. But . . . I'm not looking for any entanglements. Fact is, I'm going to be moving on soon. I've been offered a new job—a job I've been after for some time now."

Mama's eyes flickered up. They caught and held Jake's for a long moment, then she looked away. When she looked back, she had plastered a thin smile on her face.

"Well, isn't that wonderful?" she said in a falsely high voice. "Where . . . where will you be going?"

"Nevada," he said. "I'll be working at the Hoover Dam. It's a hydraulic engineering job. That's really what I've trained for."

"How nice," Mama said, her voice still strained. She rubbed her hands up and down her arms. "My, it's getting a bit chilly. Maybe . . . maybe it's not such a great night for a walk after all. Would you mind if we had that beer another time?"

27

I lay awake a long time, heartsore and bewildered. I was mad at Mama, mad at Jake, mad at Chubby, mad at myself, mad at life. How could I have made such a fool of myself? How would I ever face Jake again?

At last I fell into a fitful sleep, only to be awakened a short time later by Ginger. She was pacing back and forth on the bed and crying.

"Go to sleep, Ginger," I mumbled. But she wouldn't settle down. I opened my eyes and frowned at her. "What do you *want?*" I asked.

Immediately I noticed an odd, rosy glow in the room. I jumped up and went to the window.

"Mama!" I screamed. "Mama, come quick!"

A few minutes later, Mama stumbled into the room.

"What is it?" she asked in a worried voice.

"There's a huge fire," I cried, "over toward Greenwich Lake."

Mama bent close to the window. "Land sakes!" she whispered.

Gran padded into the room, pulling on her robe.

"What's the trouble?" she asked.

"There's a fire in the valley," Mama said.

Gran came to my side and peered out the window. "My lands!" she whispered. Then she turned and hurried out of the room.

"Where are you going?" Mama called after her.

"Outside to get a better look," said Gran.

Mama and I threw on some clothes and followed Gran downstairs and out into the night. A little cluster of neighbors had gathered at the end of our driveway, on the crest of the hill. We ran to join them.

"What is it?" Gran asked. "What's going on?"

The whole sky was orange now, and the air was thick with smoke.

"My lands," Gran repeated hoarsely as we got closer. "It looks like Armageddon!"

The great gap between Prescott Ridge and Mount Pomeroy was one huge, roiling cauldron of flame.

Aunt Stella was there and so were the Clarks. A moment later Jake came running down the driveway. He glanced at me and Mama awkwardly.

"I heard the commotion," he said. "Is everything okay?"

"Do you know what's going on?" Aunt Stella asked him.

Jake looked at us all and nodded apologetically. "They're starting the burning," he said. "They have to burn anything that might rot and pollute the water: the grasses, the trees, what's left of the buildings. . . ."

The group was silent, all eyes glued to the scene. It was

awful . . . just awful. The peaceful, green gap, where the west branch of the river used to flow, was like a vision of hell. Instinctively Mama and I moved to either side of Gran, each taking one of her arms. Her frail body trembled, the hideous flames reflected in her watery eyes.

"There are times," she whispered faintly, "when a body can live too long."

28

Jake closed up his affairs and moved out a week later. Gran seemed cheered by his leaving, but Mama and I had been mopey and irritable all week.

"Will you tell Jake good-bye for me, Celie?" Mama asked as we watched him pack up the MG through the kitchen window.

"Tell him yourself," I grumbled. "It's your fault he's leaving."

"Mine?" said Mama. "What did I have to do with it?"

"You scared him off, chasing after him like a hussy," I said. "It's no wonder he decided to get out of town."

Mama didn't answer. She just stood staring out the window for a long moment, then suddenly she turned and fled from the room.

Gran came walking in from the hall.

"Why's your mother cryin'?" she asked me.

"She's crying?" I said.

"Yes," said Gran. "Did you say something hurtful to her?"

I shrugged.

"What did you say?" Gran demanded.

"I said she was the cause of Jake leaving," I confessed.

"Now what would make you say a thing like that?" Gran asked.

"'Cause she was," I huffed, "always chasing after him. She scared him off."

Gran sniffed. "Now just listen to the pot callin' the kettle black," she said.

There was a knock on the back door and I turned. Jake pushed the door open and stepped inside the hall. He took his hat off.

"Just wanted to say good-bye," he said.

I dropped my eyes.

"Good-bye, and good luck to you," Gran said shortly.

"The same to you folks," said Jake. "Have . . . have you decided where you'll be moving yet?"

I looked at Gran.

"Don't see what concern that is of yours," she said to Jake.

"No," said Jake. "No, I guess it's not. Is . . . is Helen around?"

"She's feelin' poorly," said Gran. "Went upstairs to lie down."

"Oh," said Jake. "I'm sorry. Will you give her my best?"

"And jest what would that be?" asked Gran.

Jake looked at her quizzically. "What?" he asked.

"Just what is your *best*, Mr. Taylor," Gran asked. "What would you have me give her?"

Jake swallowed hard. "Just . . . tell her good-bye," he said.

Gran nodded.

Jake turned and caught my eye. "Bye, Celie," he said.

"Bye," I said sullenly.

"I'm . . . I'm sorry," Jake said. "I didn't mean to cause any trouble."

I blushed.

"Good-bye, Mr. Taylor," Gran repeated pointedly.

Jake opened the door.

"Good-bye," he said, "and thanks again . . . for everything."

The door banged shut with a jingle, and then we heard the engine of the MG start up. I walked through the kitchen to the dining room, watching the car rumble slowly down the driveway. I found Mama standing in the corner window of the dining room, half hidden by the draperies. Her eyes were red.

"What's wrong with you?" I asked.

She didn't answer.

"You really did fall for him, didn't you?" I said

Mama sighed. "Yes," she said, "old fool that I am."

"None of that," said Gran.

We both turned to see her standing in the doorway.

"Don't you go whippin' yourself with a switch," Gran said to Mama. "That boy'd turn the head of a plaster statue, might even'a turned mine if I were a few years younger."

Mama smiled thinly. "I actually thought he was falling for me too," she said ruefully. "Let my daydreams run away with me, I guess." She shook her head. "I ought to be old enough to know better."

"Nobody ever gets *that* old," said Gran.

Mama gave a weak laugh. "Thanks, Gran," she said. Then she sucked in a deep breath and let it out. "Well," she said, watching the MG grow smaller in the distance, "I guess it *was* too good to be true."

"What?" I asked.

Mama looked at me. "A white knight," she said, "swooping in here to rescue us all—make our lives a little easier . . . a little happier. . . ." She gazed out the window again, then she sighed deeply. "Fairy-tale endings are for others, I guess," she said. "For us, it's back to reality."

I looked over at her. "What reality?" I asked.

"Chicago," said Mama.

My heart sank.

"I called my cousin yesterday," Mama went on. "She knows of a rooming house that's clean and affordable. We'll take one room for you, Gran, and Celie and I will share another. Once we get settled and learn our way around we can look for something more permanent."

I waited for Gran's reply, expecting some kind of outburst or tirade, but her eyes just seemed to glaze over as she stood there in silence.

"We've got to contact an auction firm, Gran," Mama went on. "I think we should set the auction up for the weekend before Celie's graduation. That will give us a couple of weeks to sort things out and set aside the things we want to take with us."

Still nothing but silence.

"Gran," said Mama tiredly. "I'm sorry. I don't know what more I can say, but life has to go on, and we've got to make plans."

Gran turned and shuffled out of the room.

29

Mama woke up with a sick headache the next morning and said she couldn't go to the wedding. I knew she just couldn't face Lucille and Harry's joy. I didn't much have the heart for it, either, but Gran wouldn't hear of my staying home.

"The Thatchers and Webbers have been good friends and neighbors all our lives," she said, "and by golly we are goin' to put on a smile and celebrate Lucille and Harry's weddin' day." I put on my smile and followed Gran resolutely, vowing to think only of Lucille on this, her day.

The burning of the valley had continued through the week, and the smell of smoke lingered. A light rain overnight had cleared the air, though, and the sky was bright and blue. The whole town seemed determined to make it a happy day for Lucille and Harry. Everyone came dressed in their Sunday best, wearing their brightest smiles, laden down with gaily wrapped gifts, and carrying boxes and baskets and buckets of food. The inevitable reporters were there, too, all vying to take the best pictures and get the best quotes to write the best story about the last wedding ever to take place in the Swift River Valley.

The Webbers's front lawn was carefully mowed and clipped. The garden, where a wedding trellis had been set up, was ringed with pots of bright-colored pansies. White roses climbed the trellis and spilled from baskets on either side. Chairs had been set up on the lawn, with an aisle down the middle. There were more guests than chairs, though, so ladies were to be seated and the menfolk were to stand at the rear. A soft breeze wafted the scent of the roses through the air, and a chorus of sparrows serenaded us from the trees. The weather was so perfect one almost wondered if God had taken pity on our poor, devastated valley and designed this day for us as a parting gift.

Gran and I took our seats, and Aunt Stella sat down beside us.

Lucille's Scottish uncle came out in full regalia and began to play his bagpipe, a sound so sweet it brought tears to my eyes before the bride even made her appearance. When all was in readiness, he struck up the wedding march, and we all turned toward the house. The maid of honor came out of the house dressed in a sleek gown of lavender satin. She walked down the steps of the Webbers's front porch followed by three bridesmaids, all dressed in lavender and wearing crowns of baby's breath. Then came Lucille's little cousin Meredith in a froth of pale green chiffon, dropping rose petals from a white wicker basket. At last, on the arm of her father, came Lucille. She wore the gown that her mother had worn, and her grandmother before her. It was beautiful, antique satin, with a high neck and long, pearl-encrusted sleeves. She wore a simple pearl circlet upon her brow, with a long train of lace flowing out behind.

She beamed with joy, and I was happy for her, but sad, too, missing Jake and thinking that my own dream of being married at home, here in our valley, would never come true. The ceremony was bittersweet, with not a few tears shed, and I think it was a relief to us all when Reverend Marsh finally pronounced the two man and wife and the fiddle players rosined up their bows and livened things up with a jig.

I retreated to the Webber kitchen to help Gran and Aunt Stella and some of the other ladies with the food. I would have been content to hide there all day, but Chubby came looking for me, and Aunt Stella shooed me out to "have some fun."

I followed Chubby out to the yard and we got into line for the food.

"So, I hear lover-boy's gone," said Chubby.

"Shut up, Chubby," I said.

Before us was a spread as fine as any wedding the valley had ever seen—fried chicken, country ham, roast beef and turkey, all kinds of cheeses, hot biscuits, sausage and gravy. There was every kind of salad and casserole imaginable, baked beans, corn fritters, and hot loaves of bread.

For dessert there were five different kinds of pie, plates piled with homemade cookies, tins of fudge and home-pulled taffy, and a mile-high wedding cake baked by Lucille's mother and decorated by her uncle, a pastry chef from Springfield.

Suddenly, though, I had no appetite. I put my plate down and walked away.

"Hey," said Chubby, following after me. "What's the matter?"

"Nothing," I said.

I sat down on the stone wall at the edge of the lawn. Chubby sat down next to me.

"Why don't you just go eat," I said, "before they run out."

"Fat chance of that," said Chubby. "They got food enough there to feed King Kong. Besides, I'm not going anywhere till you tell me what's eating *you?*"

"Nothing," I insisted, but the next thing I knew, tears sprang to my eyes. I wiped them away quickly so the other wedding guests wouldn't see.

"Jeesh," said Chubby. "You really were stuck on that guy, weren't you?"

"No!" I snapped. "It's just . . . never mind."

I got up and stalked off across the backyard and down the hill toward Beaver Brook.

Chubby followed.

"Leave me alone!" I cried over my shoulder when we were out of earshot of the crowd.

But Chubby stayed right with me. At last he grabbed my arm and whirled me around.

"Hey," he said, "I'm sorry about teasing you, okay? I didn't know that guy meant that much to you."

I put my free hand up and rubbed my eyes.

"He didn't," I said, "or maybe he did. I don't know. I'm so confused, Chubby. Everything is such a mess."

"What?" Chubby asked. "What's a mess?"

"Our lives," I said. "We're leaving, Chubby. Mama took that job in Chicago, and we're leaving right after graduation."

Chubby's jaw dropped. "What?" he said. "When did she decide that?"

"Sometime this week. She told Gran last night."

"And what did Gran say?"

"She didn't say anything. And that worries me too. She's just not herself lately."

"Look," said Chubby, "if your grandmother hasn't agreed, nothing is settled yet. Things could still change."

I shook my head. "I don't think so. Mama's already rented a room for us, and she's hiring an auctioneer this week."

Chubby put his hands in his pockets and leaned back against a big maple tree. He stared up at the canopy of deep green leaves.

"That stinks," he said, his voice unusually husky. "That just plain lousy stinks."

30

The next two weeks were filled with packing and sorting and planning, all of which I did with a heavy heart, and none of which Gran took a hand in. She continued on like nothing was happening around her, puttering in her kitchen garden, canning rhubarb and snow peas, chasing down the winter's cobwebs with her feather duster and broom. I would see her glance out of the corner of her eye, though, at a piece of furniture Mama and I had pulled out into the hall, or a pile of china dishes on the dining room sideboard, and as she moved on I would hear a weighty sigh. She gave up eating almost entirely, and she looked frailer and smaller each day until I began to fear, if this went on much longer, that she would simply fade away.

On Friday of the second week the auction company came in and moved all the furniture and boxes out to the dairy barn and the carriage house. Ginger ran from room to room, hiding under beds and on top of bureaus and wardrobes only to have each new hiding place snatched away. She scurried beneath the feet of the movers, looking frightened and bewildered. At last she took refuge in the only room that remained untouched—Gran's.

"Gran," said Mama, when the moving was almost done, "there are some pieces we need to take out of your room."

"No," said Gran.

"But we can't take it with us, Gran," Mama said more gently. "We just can't."

"No," said Gran again, and she walked away.

Mama looked at me and sighed. "We can wait one more day," she said, "but her things have to go into the auction on Sunday. Maybe you can talk some sense into her, Celie."

"No," I said quietly. "It doesn't make sense to me, either."

Mama grimaced in frustration and stalked off to oversee the movers.

By evening the house seemed like a foreign place. Most of the rooms were empty, the curtains were down, and the walls were decorated only with deeper-toned rectangles where pictures used to hang. Our voices echoed through the empty rooms with a hollow *twang* and the sound of our footsteps thudded dully off the blank walls. It was happening. *Someday* was really happening. I took Ginger to bed with me and cried myself to sleep.

Saturday dawned clear and breezy, and the auctioneer set up his platform outdoors between the two barns. The auction was scheduled to begin at ten o'clock, but by eight A.M. folks were already drifting into the yard and milling around the barns.

"Look at 'em," snapped Gran, "all chompin' at the bit to cash in on someone else's misery, hopin' they'll get a bargain out of the deal." She marched out to the auctioneer's platform. "Mind you get a fair price," she said, shaking a finger at him. "I'd sooner give my things away than see 'em go to some bargain hunter that's gonna turn around and sell 'em to some poor unsuspectin' soul for twice what they're worth."

Behind Gran's back, Mama was motioning the man to disregard Gran's instructions.

"I'll do the best I can, ma'am," the man promised diplomatically.

By ten o'clock there must've been a couple hundred people in the crowd, mostly strangers, but a few valley people too. Aunt Stella was there, and Chubby, of course, and his family, and Lucille and Harry, hoping to pick up a few things for their new home in Belchertown. The Clarks were there, too, mainly out of curiosity, I think, and a handful of other friends and neighbors.

Gran dragged a wooden rocker out onto the back porch and sat down where she could keep an eye on the proceedings. Aunt Stella brought out a kitchen chair and sat next to her. Chubby and I sat on the steps by their feet.

The auctioneer began with a small occasional table that used to stand in our parlor.

"This is a lovely piece in the Sheraton style," he said, "solid cherry, with an ivory inlay. Let's start the bidding with five dollars."

"Five dollars!" Gran jumped up. "That table's almost a hunert years old! It's worth twenty-five dollars if it's worth a dime!"

The auctioneer looked at Gran, then he looked at Mama, who shrugged helplessly.

"All right then," the auctioneer said. "We'll start the bidding at twenty-five dollars. Twenty-five dollars, anyone?"

Nobody raised a hand.

"Twenty-five," the auctioneer repeated, "do I hear twenty-five?"

Still no hands.

"How about twenty?" said the auctioneer. "Do I hear twenty?"

Gran slowly sank back down into her chair and the price sank with her. Twenty. Fifteen. Ten. Five. At last, at three dollars someone raised a hand, then another bid three fifty, and it finally sold for four. Gran's face was contorted in rage.

"Bloody cheapskates," she muttered.

The next item was a chest of drawers, and once again Gran leaped to her feet in protest over the opening bid. Mama stomped over.

"Gran," she said, "all you're doing is slowing things down. This man knows what he's doing and he's getting the best price he can."

"It's robbery," Gran snapped.

Aunt Stella patted her hand. "Helen's right, Liz," she said, "best to let them get on with it."

Gran pressed her lips into a thin, white line and sank back down into her chair. She said nothing more, just rocked and glared, rocked and glared as the auctioneer held up one piece of our lives after another and auctioned them all off to the highest bidder. The dearer an object was to Gran's heart, the harder she rocked.

"You're gonna wear a hole clear through the porch floor, Lizzie," said Aunt Stella.

"Don't matter. They're gonna tear it down anyway," Gran grumbled.

At noontime, the auctioneer took a break, and Mama went inside and called us all for dinner. Gran refused to budge, and when Aunt Stella took a biscuit and a piece of fried chicken out to her, she threw it to a stray dog that had wandered in with the crowd.

Mama shook her head in exasperation.

"Do you see what I put up with?" she said when Aunt Stella came back in.

Aunt Stella looked at Gran through the kitchen window. "It's hard on her," she said with a sigh.

"It's hard on us all," said Mama.

"Yes . . . but harder on the old," Aunt Stella said sadly, "much harder on the old."

Soon after dinner the auctioneer started up again, and Aunt Stella had to leave. Her nephew was coming by with his truck to pick up some furniture she was giving him.

"When are you actually moving, Aunt Stella?" I asked.

"First of the month, dear," she replied. "I'll be around for a while yet."

"That's good," I said.

Chubby and I went back outside and sat on a rock in the shade of the old sycamore. I picked up a stick and scratched aimlessly in the dirt. The auctioneer brought out our old grandfather clock, and a lump came to my throat.

"You doin' okay?" Chubby asked me.

I nodded, but tears had been bottled up just behind my

eyes all day and now one slipped by. I brushed it away and sniffed.

"This may sound dumb," I said, staring at the clock, "but when I was little I thought that clock was the grandfather of all the other clocks in the house, and since I didn't have a grandfather of my own, I pretended that it was my grandfather too. In the night when I'd wake and hear the chimes, I'd feel like my grandfather was watching over me, and it would make me feel safe."

"I don't think that's dumb at all," said Chubby. "Maybe it will go to a house where there is another little girl, and in the night it will comfort her too."

I smiled thinly. "And who will comfort me?" I asked.

Chubby squeezed my hand.

"I wish I could," he said.

"You'll be a million miles away," I told him dejectedly.

The bidding on the clock was over. A tall man had gotten it. He and another man carried it out to a truck that was parked back on the street. Gran rocked furiously as they went by. Poor Gran. It seemed like everyone who carried something away carried a piece of her soul with it. By day's end, I was afraid she'd be nothing but a hollow shell.

There was a loud scraping sound and I turned to see four men dragging the sleigh out of the carriage house.

"Oh no," I said, jumping up.

"What?" asked Chubby.

"My grandfather proposed to Gran in that sleigh," I said. "This is going to kill her. I've got to go to her."

I pushed through the crowd and got to Gran's side just as the bidding began.

"C'mon, Gran," I said. "Let's go inside for a while."

"No," said Gran, but she was trembling.

I looked at the auction platform. The sleigh sat just below it, and a number of people were bidding against one another for it.

"But you're shivering, Gran," I said.

"Just took a chill, that's all," said Gran. "Leave me be."

The bidding was up to twenty dollars, going back and forth between a couple of men who looked like farmers. Then suddenly someone called out, "forty dollars."

I strained to see, but whoever had bid was lost in the crowd.

The auctioneer looked surprised.

"Forty dollars," he repeated. "Do I hear forty-one?"

The crowd was silent.

"Forty going once," said the auctioneer. "Forty going twice. *Sold* to the man in the red plaid shirt."

I watched as the man in the red plaid shirt came forward.

"It's Chubby's dad!" I cried.

Gran's eyes widened.

Chubby came bursting through the crowd, grinning from ear to ear.

"We got it!" he cried. "My dad is going to use it as an ornament out in front of the new station. Ma's gonna fill it with different flowers every season." He paused and looked down at Gran. "Ma thought that might be pleasing to you, Mrs. Wheeler," he said.

Gran nodded, her eyes shiny with tears.

"Chubby, you're the best," I said, stretching up to plant a kiss on his cheek.

31

Gran hardly touched her dinner. She seemed beaten down with exhaustion. She didn't even object when Mama told her to go into the parlor and sit while we washed up the dishes. I went in to check on her as soon as we were done. Her frail little body seemed lost on her overstuffed chair. Her head was back and her eyes were closed. The radio was playing softly.

"You okay, Gran?" I asked.

She nodded slowly.

Mama came in and looked down at her apologetically. "Gran," she said, "I know how tired you are, but we've really got to go up and sort out the things in your room."

"No," said Gran quietly.

Mama sighed and bent down next to Gran.

"Gran," she said gently. "We just *can't* take it all to Chicago."

Gran opened her eyes. "I'm not going to Chicago," she said.

Mama turned and gave me a pleading look.

"Please, Gran," I begged. "You belong with us, wherever we are."

Gran looked over at me and managed a smile. "I'll always be with you, wherever you are, dear," she said. "But I can't go to Chicago."

Mama shook her head. "You don't belong in a home, Gran," she said.

"I don't b'long in Chicago, either," Gran replied firmly.

"What are we going to do with you?" asked Mama in exasperation.

"Just let me set here and listen to my program in peace," said Gran.

Mama gave up and walked out of the room, and Gran put her head back and closed her eyes again. Kate Smith was on the radio, singing with Miller's orchestra.

I slumped down on the couch. "Gran?" I said.

Gran waved her hand. "Not now, darlin'," she said tiredly. "Just let me rest a bit."

I gave up, too, and sat quietly, lost in my own thoughts, until Gran fell asleep. I got up and switched channels, then curled up on the couch to listen to the *Green Hornet*. When it went off at nine o'clock, Mama came back in.

"Bedtime," she said. "We all have a busy day tomorrow."

"What are we going to do about Gran's room?" I whispered.

Mama shook her head. "I guess we'll figure that out in the morning." She went over and patted Gran's shoulder gently. "Bedtime, Gran," she said.

Gran's head lolled forward, but her eyes didn't open. "Gran," said Mama, a bit more loudly, but Gran still didn't wake. Mama stared at her oddly, then suddenly she dropped to her knees and put her ear to Gran's chest. I froze.

"Gran?" I screamed.

Mama pulled back and grabbed Gran's two hands in hers. She held them a long moment, then slowly she pitched forward and lay her head on Gran's lap.

"Oh, Gran," she said, her voice breaking. "You stubborn old woman. You stubborn, stubborn old woman."

32

We buried Gran between Grandfather and Daddy. Doc Seaver said the cause of death was heart failure. Maybe that was how she died, but I knew it wasn't why she died. She died because the people in Boston killed her, and I hated them for it.

I stood in silence as Reverend Marsh read the Bible over Gran's coffin. Mama sniffled beside me, but I wouldn't look at her, wouldn't let her touch me. This was her fault, too, making Gran sell all her beloved things, making her choose between Chicago and a home. I wanted her to hurt, wanted her to feel as much pain as she had caused Gran.

The cemetery was filled with friends and neighbors. They had come from far and near, many of whom I hadn't seen in years, some I'd never met—people who grew up with Gran, people who went to school with her, neighbors, friends from the Quabbin Club, people who worked with her on various charities, or on the town council, people who'd respected her, people who'd loved her.

When we got back to the house, it was filled to bursting—filled with people, filled with noise, filled with food, but empty all the same without Gran. I didn't feel like talking to anyone, not even to Chubby. I went up and sulked in my room, cuddling with Ginger. After a while Mama came up, but I wouldn't talk to her, wouldn't let her near me.

"You broke her heart," I said. "Leave me alone."

She went away quietly, with tears in her eyes.

A few minutes later Aunt Stella barged in.

"Go away," I said. "I don't want to talk to anybody."

"Well, you're goin' to," said Aunt Stella, "whether you want to or not."

"You can't make me," I said.

"Maybe not," she agreed, "but I can give you a piece of my mind, at least."

"Me?" I cried in astonishment. "What have I done?"

"You're treating your mama shameful," said Aunt Stella. "I won't have it."

I frowned. "She deserves it," I said.

"For what?" asked Aunt Stella. "For raising you up all these years, feeding you, clothing you, sittin' up with you when you were sick, lovin' you to death?"

I didn't answer.

"Celie," she said, shaking a finger at me, "your mama had nothin' to do with your grandmother's death. I don't ever want to hear you say such a thing to her again."

"But she—"

"I'm not finished," Aunt Stella interrupted. "Your grandmother died of a broken heart. She died because this valley was so much a part of her she wasn't whole without it."

"But Mama made it worse," I protested. "We could have moved close by, could have kept a lot of Gran's things."

"Wouldn't matter," said Aunt Stella. "Wasn't the things she couldn't part with. It was the spirits in this house, here on this land. It was the community. It was havin' them all around her that made her strong."

I looked at my daddy's old milking pail, sitting with a pile of my belongings in the corner of the room.

"But things help," I said. "They're better than nothing."

Aunt Stella nodded. "Maybe so," she said, "but it was your grandmother's time to go, Celie. It was the way she wanted it."

Tears welled up inside me and spilled over. "But, why?" I cried. "Why would she leave me?"

Aunt Stella pulled me into her arms. "Oh darlin', she didn't leave you," she whispered. "She never will. But it was time for her to let you go. I know you don't understand that now, but I promise you, in time, you will."

I found Mama out on the porch swing, her face tear-streaked and puffy, a handkerchief twisted in her hands. I went over and sat down beside her. She turned and searched my face. "Sorry, Mama," I whispered, then tears sprang anew to my eyes and we fell into each other's arms.

33

I t is *someday*. Graduation Day—June 22, 1938.

Miss Rourke wants the graduates there an hour early, so Chubby's parents pick me up and drive the two of us into town. Enfield is a pitiful sight, nothing left now but the post office, the town hall, Haskell's General Store, Miller's filling station, and the school building. The hills in the distance are brown and bare, and the landscape all around is a dusty, dirty desert.

The MDWSC is letting us have graduation in the town hall because the schoolhouse is too small to accommodate all the friends and neighbors and, of course, the reporters who will be attending. We decorate the stage with flowers and ferns and evergreens to try to brighten things up and take people's minds off the bleak landscape outside, but for me, especially, it is not enough to dispel the gloom. Mama and I are leaving for Chicago this afternoon.

There are only seven of us graduating, so we sit on the stage, three on one side of the podium, four on the other. Chubby and I sit next to each other, watching as the crowd files in. Mama and Aunt Stella sit down side by side in the front row and smile up at us proudly, but Gran's absence is like a hole in the air.

Some-out-of-towner named Mr. Garner, a high-ranking person from the grange, is the speaker. Lost in my thoughts, I don't hear a word he says. I keep seeing Gran out of the corner of my eye, sitting prim and proud beside Mama, with her ankles crossed and her purse clutched in her gloved hands. I can even smell her lavender perfume. Each time I turn to look at her, it comes as a jolt all over again to see that she isn't really there.

Finally, the speech ends, and Mr. Cicione, the principal, says a few words, then Doc Seaver gives us our diplomas and we march out to a scratchy recording of "Pomp and Circumstance."

There is a reception outside in the schoolyard, with cookies and punch. People mill around making small talk. No one is eager to leave. This is it, the final event. Most everyone is moving after today. As the afternoon wears on, though, folks inevitably begin to drift away, parting after tearful parting. It is even hard to say good-bye to Belinda. We promise to write, though I know we probably never will.

Aunt Stella hugs me to her bosom and dabs at her eyes with a lace hanky.

"You write to me, now, you hear?" she says. "And you come back and see me when you can."

"I will, Aunt Stella," I promise, sniffing back tears.

Mama looks at her watch. "Tom will be here shortly to

drive us into Springfield to the bus station," she tells me. "You and Chubby had better say your good-byes."

I look at Chubby and swallow down the huge lump that rises in my throat. I have put this moment off as long as I can. It can't be put off anymore. I nod to Chubby and, silently, we walk to the edge of the millpond and sit on the bench where we've sat so many noontimes over the years, eating our butter and sugar sandwiches and drinking lukewarm milk from a mason jar. We stare out upon our scorched and desolate valley.

"Hard to believe that before long it's going to be a lake," says Chubby.

I nod.

"Someday people might picnic up there in the hills," he says, "and never know about us, never know that our whole world was once down here, under the water."

"It isn't fair," I say, dabbing at my teary eyes with my handkerchief.

Chubby murmurs in agreement.

I sniff hard, turning my hanky to try to find a dry spot. "I feel like I've cried enough tears this year to fill the reservoir myself," I say.

"I know," says Chubby, rolling his eyes. "I had to dry most of them."

I can't help but laugh. "What am I going to do without you, Chubby?" I ask.

Chubby bends in that familiar way to kiss me on the forehead. Only this time he bends farther and kisses me fully on the lips. His kiss is soft and sweet and stirring, and I don't pull away. When the kiss is over, I look at him in surprise.

"What was that?" I ask.

Chubby blushes and drops his eyes. "That bull thing, I guess," he says.

I smile. "No, really."

He looks up at me and blushes even more deeply. "I . . . I love you, Celie," he stammers. "I always have. Not just like a friend, but like a boy. I know you're too torn up inside to feel much of anything right now, but I'm hoping maybe *someday* . . . you'll realize that you love me too."

Someday. That word again. Strange, I think as Chubby gathers me in his arms . . . strange how that one word can signal both an ending, and a new beginning.

Tom arrives with Ginger and our bags already loaded into the Model T. I climb in and slump down in the seat, feeling empty, all cried out. Chubby throws a kiss, then he waves and waves, running alongside the car until we leave him in the dust. I wave, too, until we begin climbing Great Quabbin Hill and I can't see him anymore. The Model T rumbles past our house, standing empty and forlorn, and I find that I'm not all cried out after all. Mama reaches over the back of the front seat, takes my hand, and squeezes it. Her brow is creased with worry, and I realize how big a step this is for her, for both of us.

I squeeze back. "I'll be okay, Mama," I say. "We'll be okay."

She smiles and nods, with tear-rimmed eyes.

Ginger mews unhappily in her carrier on the seat beside me. I dab my eyes and glance around me, still sensing Gran's presence, still smelling her lavender scent, even above the noxious fumes of the Model T.

"Are you wearing Gran's perfume?" I ask Mama.

"No," she says, "why?"

"Just wondering," I murmur, but I am not wondering any-more. Gran is with me, I realize, just as she promised she would be.

Up ahead, the world is fresh and green; behind us, scorched and brown. As Tom swings the car west toward Springfield, I turn back for one last look. The MDWSC tells us the valley will be lovely again someday, an oasis of peace and natural beauty. I can't see that now, can't see what some-day holds for the valley, or for me. But I know one thing. My roots sink deep into the soil of this valley, deeper than any earth machine can dig, and through whatever lies ahead, they will sustain me.

AUTHOR'S NOTE

Today the Quabbin Reservoir is a pristine, sparkling body of water where eagles nest and countless varieties of plant and animal wildlife flourish. Little Quabbin Hill, Mount Pomeroy, Mount Ram, and many of the other former mountains are islands now, rising up out of the water like great green gumdrops. The largest body of untreated drinking water in the country, the Quabbin holds 412 billion gallons of water and serves Boston and most of eastern Massachusetts.

To the handful of displaced residents who meet on Tuesday afternoons in what is now the Metropolitan District Water Commission building at the reservoir's edge, though, it is still home. In their seventies and eighties now, they represent the last of the more than 2,000 residents who were forced from the valley when the towns of Enfield, Dana, Prescott, and Greenwich were taken by eminent domain in 1938. Though their numbers have dwindled over the years, they remain a community, held together by their memories and their sense of belonging to one another. If you ask, they will tell you their stories, and when they reach the part about leaving the valley, some will still get tears in their eyes. It is this deep love of the land, this deep sense of community that I wanted to capture in writing *Someday*. I think these things are lacking in our society today, and I think we may miss them more than we know.

Celie Wheeler and her family and friends are fictitious, but the events they lived through are real. The Swift River Act was indeed passed in 1928 and the MDWSC began buying up properties immediately. As depicted, though, many families rode out the Depression by renting their homes back from the commission at very reasonable rates and staying on in the valley.

The final notices did go out in February 1938, and people were asked to leave by April 1. People with children in school or other pressing reasons were allowed to stay longer, though. Demolition moved into high gear in the spring of 1938 and culminated in the burning of the valley, to which many of the last residents bore witness. (In some cases events have been compressed in time to fit into the span of this book.)

The farewell ball was indeed held on April 27, and its description is based on newspaper accounts of the event. Although I've fictionalized their last names and the description of their wedding, a couple named Lucille and Harry were indeed the last ones to be married in the valley, and the event did take place outside on their lawn on June 30, 1938.

Many of the fictional characters in the book are based on real people, but since I did not know them, I chose not to use their real names. Benjamin Rowan, quoted at the ball, was a real person, and his words are an actual quote taken from the book *The Day Four Quabbin Towns Died*, by J. R. Greene.

The post office, the last one in the valley, was really in Enfield, as was the town hall, the school, the grange, the filling station, the meat market, the dry goods store, and the millpond. The post office closed on January 14, 1939, and the flooding began on August 14 of the same year. It took seven years for the valley to fill.

The town of Warton is fictitious but representative of any number of the small surrounding towns to which many valley residents moved.

There has always been controversy over whether it was fair to take land in western Massachusetts to slake the growing thirst of a sprawling, metropolitan Boston. Some former residents remained embittered about it until their deaths. Others were more philosophical and forgiving.

Right or wrong, the past is past. The real question is, could it ever happen again? There is no doubt that the availability of clean drinking water will continue to be an issue in the next century and beyond, but it is unlikely that a land grab the size of the Quabbin will ever be tolerated again. Today the opposition would be stronger and more organized. The people are more aware of their rights and have more resources available to them to help protect those rights. New, more creative approaches to water acquisition must be and are being explored, like seawater conversion, conservation through repair of leaking pipes and aqueducts, installation of water-saving devices, and heightened consumer awareness. The days of cheap water, like the days of cheap power, are numbered in this country. Prices have gone up and will continue to rise, and this in itself will encourage conservation, eventually forcing consumers to make conservation a priority. Had many of these measures been taken earlier on, could the Swift River Valley have been spared? Possibly, but at this point, if you'll pardon the expression, that is water over the dam.

Parts of the Quabbin Reservoir are open to the public today for hiking, bird-watching, canoeing, and other environmentally friendly pursuits. The watershed is still dotted with old foundations, doorsteps, stone walls, hitching posts, and other reminders of the past. It is a beautiful, peaceful place, and one need only walk down the old lanes, through the old fields, across the old greens, to know that Gran's words were true. The people are still there. You can feel their spirits all around you, slipping through the dappled shadows, whispering in the wind, soaring on eagle's wings over the shining waters, keeping an ever watchful eye upon this gentle valley that they called home.

BIBLIOGRAPHY

Conuel, Thomas. *Quabbin: The Accidental Wilderness*. Amherst, Mass.: University of Massachusetts Press, 1981. Revised 1990.

Greene, J. R. *An Atlas of the Quabbin Valley and Ware River Diversion*. Athol, Mass.: J&P Printing, 1996.

_____*The Creation of the Quabbin Reservoir*. Athol, Mass.: The Transcript Press, 1981.

_____*The Day Four Quabbin Towns Died*. Athol, Mass.: The Transcript Press, 1985

Howell, Donald. *Quabbin: The Lost Valley*, Ware, Mass.: Quabbin Book House, 1951.

Letters from the Quabbin. The Friends of Quabbin, Belchertown, Massachusetts.

Metropolitan District Commission Quabbin Visitor Center and Friends of the Quabbin. *Here Was Home*, an audio history of the Swift River Valley and Quabbin Reservoir, 1995.

A wealth of additional information is available at the Quabbin Visitor Center at the Quabbin Reservoir.

JACKIE FRENCH KOLLER is the author of many novels, chapter books, and picture books, including *Bouncing on the Bed*, *The Dragonling*, *The Falcon*, and *A Place to Call Home*. She lives in Westfield, Massachusetts, with her husband, George, and their two dogs.